THE BAKU

Edward Bryant (signature)

This signed edition is limited to
500 numbered and 26 lettered copies.

This is copy _188_ .

THE
BAKU

THE
BAKU TALES OF THE NUCLEAR AGE

Edward Bryant

SUBTERRANEAN PRESS ✱ 2001

First Edition

The Baku: Tales of the Nuclear Age
Copyright © 2001 by Edward Bryant

"Jody After the War" Copyright © 1972 by Edward Bryant, originally appeared in *Orbit 10* edited by Damon Knight (Putnam).

"The *Hibakusha* Gallery" Copyright © 1977 by Edward Bryant, originally appeared in Penthouse, June 1977.

"The Baku" Copyright © 1987 by Edward Bryant, originally appeared in *Night Visions 4* (Dark Harvest Press).

Cover Copyright © 2001 by David Martin.
Interior Design Copyright © 2001 by Tim Holt.

"The Twilight Zone" is a registered trademark of CBS, Inc.

ISBN
1-892284-52-9

Subterranean Press
PO Box 190106
Burton, MI 48519

e-mail:
publisher@subterraneanpress.com

Website:
www.subterraneanpress.com

DEDICATION

For Jo, my love and energy to a survivor without compare.

I owe abundant thanks to many people who helped make sure this peculiar but dear-to-me book come about: Certainly there are the *Twilight Zone* people who gave me the ill-fated script assignment...Phil, Harlan, Jim, George, Joe, Rock, Alan, and the rest. But of them all, it was Harlan whose perhaps ill-placed faith carried me through. And George, who did what he could do to be a good friend. Thanks to Mary Rita who supplied my first experience with an incredibly expensive laptop; and Darren who gave me a place to write the script undisturbed (and do you still have that signed Jerzy Kosinski???). I owe Paul and Scot profuse thanks for allowing me the privilege of publishing the prose version of this story in their Night Visions series (I'll never forget the morning I thought Paul was going to beat the crap out of me just outside Denver's Union Station — but that's another story). A tip of the old Army Air Corps hat to Lucy who discovered and wrote about the *baku* about the same time I did. Thanks to Frank D., who shared the same dark, grotesque dreams of flash and ashes as yours truly. And to Damon whose heart melted for good reason. Monumental thanks to Bill whose patience and good humor saw this book reach publication, as well as to David, for his fabulous panoramic art. And enormous affection and gratitude to Dawn who saw to it I lived long enough to complete this project. But my final acknowledgment must of course be to the *hibakusha*, the survivors of all disasters, all holocausts throughout humanity's frequently inhuman history. If pain and nightmare, death and oblivion, can in any way metamorphose to compassion and healing — or at least galvanize it in others, then perhaps a small portion of your suffering may receive some balm.

INTRODUCTION:
NOBODY KNOWS ANYTHING

Hey, I thought *I* knew something about Hollywood when Harlan finessed a pitch session for me in front of the staff of CBS's revival of the classic Rod Serling series, *The Twilight Zone*. Turned out, William Goldman was right. Nobody knows anything. Least of all me.

That was back in the '80s. By then I'd adapted one of my own stories as a pilot for a *Twilight Zone* knockoff on the Disney Channel. The pilot was shot and endlessly telecast but the series was never picked up. I'd had stories optioned and adapted by others. "While She Was Out" eventually ended up as a nifty production on Lifetime Cable's *The Hidden Room*, starring Stephanie Zimbalist as my hero.

Earlier, a hot young director named Frank DePalma had loved my story "The *Hibakusha* Gallery" in *Penthouse* and had secured permission to shoot it as a short feature. It was a senior student project at UCLA, to be sure, but it was a conscientious, eerily gorgeous, definitely disturbing, thoroughly professional piece of work. Dealing with many of the same issues as "The Baku," The 30-minute version of "The *Hibakusha* Gallery" made it all the way up the Oscar ladder to the cut just below the finalists for best short feature.

It's a story that started out with a single visual image, the boardwalk photo gallery that's the centerpiece of the story. I wrote about two thousand words setting everything up. Then I stalled for two and a half years before I finished it. I believe it was a matter of having to let my skills catch up with my ambition.

The other included story of postnuclear survival, "Jody After the War," was bought by Damon Knight for his original anthology *Orbit 10*. Damon, at heart a softy—sort of—is known for a certain sternness of outward sensibility. Legend has it he's one hard-nosed editor. Damon told me in his acceptance that if "Jody" got him in the heart as it had, it ought to melt down the average sf reader.

So they're all in this volume, a short but peculiar sequence of thematically connected works.

Now back to our regularly scheduled title story and its cautionary journey.

It's the logical extension of my long, strange apprenticeship in L.A. when for most of four years in the late '60s and early '70s, I lived as a houseguest in the home of Harlan Ellison. My valued mentor then (and still, actually), my wonderful friend for more than three decades now, Harlan had tried to teach me how the Hollywood system worked. In that regard, I probably wasn't as good a student as he could have hoped.

But I've always wanted to write for the screen. And why not? I had a typewriter, plenty of paper, a fresh ribbon, and the delusion I was talented! Then there were the thousands of hours of TV and the two or three zillion movies, good, bad, and lousy I'd watched over my childhood and young adult years. I knew I could write that stuff.

Dissolve to the mid-eighties. Harlan was working on the story staff of the new *Twilight Zone* series, the brainchild of producer Phil Deguerre. It was a credible version; I suspect Rod Serling, most of the time, was not rolling in his grave.

Harlan's a generous writer who tries to offer breaks to younger, ambitious writers. So he got me a story conference with the *TZ* staff. He told me how to prepare. He suggested how to dress. The preparation involved putting together six or eight story springboards for possible episodes. One or two should be deliberate dogs, easy targets for the staff to shoot down. That'd make selling one of the good ideas easier.

Dressing for success involved the "prince from a distant land" look. I was a published author; that stood in my favor. I was flying in from Colorado; that was also good. I should wear a decent dark sport jacket, an open-collared shirt, and brand-new razor-creased jeans.

Pitch sessions were invented as a torturer's delight by the most inventively sadistic minions of hell. Just because *your entire career* appears to hinge on being able to sell an idea to a group of industry professionals, and that an integral skill is being able to field absolutely out-of-left-weird-field plot suggestions and instantly incorporate them into your premise without totally negating your bright idea...hey, cake. Right? Some people delight in the games aspect, the very challenge of pitching. Others panic. Like me.

It wasn't that I was completely a virgin. I'd pitched in previous years to the likes of Philip Barry, the legendary creator of *The Philadelphia Story*, and to Ralph Bakshi for the gig writing *Fire and Ice*. I'd bombed out in all cases.

So now I got my story premises together. And no, I didn't practice in front of the mirror. Harlan had assured me I wouldn't be facing that tough a house. After all, I already *knew* most of these guys.

Whatever. It was a blur. I do remember Phil the producer stopping me in the middle of one pitch because something I'd said had reminded him of an item he'd heard was in that day's *L.A. Times*. He interrupted me in mid-sentence, begged my indulgence, and called in his secretary to pick up a paper for him, and then smiled and urged me to resume the pitch.

The short of it was I somehow managed to get through the hour. The climax was the staff warming to one story springboard, something I called "The Baku."

So I got the assignment, Writer's Guild minimum rates, a contract, everything. Riches were here; fame would come. All we needed was the script. No problem.

But I couldn't do it. Call it flop sweat. To me the stakes seemed sufficiently high to warrant freezing up. Weeks slipped past toward the increasingly tight deadline. I eventually realized I'd have to do the draft extremely fast; as it turned out, in the 72 hours or so after I was the guest of honor at an east coast science fiction convention.

Generous friends chipped in to help me out, offering a state-of-the-art (for that time) laptop (thank you, Mary Rita), setting me up in a quiet Washington D.C. condo (thank you, Darren). And I wrote the script.

I wrote it and printed it out (no e-mail attachments back then) and overnighted it in. And waited.

One night the *TZ* staff phoned me in Denver on a conference call. There was a speakerphone in the production office. All the guys were there. They were not angry, I realized later. They all sounded regretful, extremely sad. Especially Harlan. Well...he sounded the closest to angry. The tone of his voice was not entirely cordial the next day when he called me privately and asked whether I had just shined on the script. I couldn't blame him.

To say that everyone hated the script would be the blandest of understatements. They hated it so virulently, there was no chance of okaying a second draft to work out the problems of the first. This was in spite of the story having a premise everyone had apparently loved.

They were right.

The script was dead. Stone dead. Dead on arrival. And no, I'll spoil the suspense. That terrifyingly inept effort is not the script you've shelled out good money for in order to buy this book.

In my own head beaten by Hollywood—and myself—my tale (and metaphoric tail) tucked maybe permanently between my legs, I was ready to pack it in. No more dreams of big-time tinsel.

Then I had an idea. It could have worked as a story springboard, maybe even for *The Twilight Zone* itself. Or a Frank Capra movie. I called my old buddy George R.R. Martin who was, of course, one of the brightest stars shining in the firmament of my generation of sf writers. He was still on staff at *TZ*.

I know I can't write a new draft of the script under the basic rules, I said to him. But I'd like to try reworking it informally. Unpaid. Unauthorized. And if I do that, I implored George, will you take a look at the result? If the new version is on the level of what I should have done the first time around, would you consider interceding with the rest of the staff and letting them know I finally came through? That I'm not a complete loser? That I coulda been a contender?

Probably fearing I'd come out to Hollywood with meat-ax and a crazed look in my eyes if he turned me down, George very kindly said yes.

So I took my lousy script and started over.

I finished it, let it steep, edited it, and then sent it off to George.

It arrived the week CBS cancelled the series.

Oh, well.

So now years have gone by and I'm finally pulling the draft out of the closet the way a guy tugs a dusty tarp off a once favorite but now half-remembered bike.

I'm not saying this alternative version of the Baku script is all that good. But boy, you should have seen the one that slunk away! Which reminds me—I've got to burn the final copy of the first draft before I die and it becomes something like my very own Islands in the Stream, only far more damning. My reputation's already got dramatic tire tracks across its chest; it doesn't need a thick wooden stake through the heart.

So enjoy. Do the obligatory compare-and-contrast analysis of prose and script. You don't have to be kind.

Oh, and did I tell you? Well, I'm working on a new project for the screen. Sort of like Jean Shepherd meets Clive Barker. And with my luck, as directed by Renny Harlin or Roland Emmerich.

See you at the movies.

Edward Bryant
April 2000
Denver

THE BAKU

Whatever it was, it sucked at him—not like a maelstrom tugging at his body, but rather something unspeakable syphoning the deepest pools of his mind. Somehow he knew it was feeding on him. What it drank, he didn't know. He had only the knowledge that something had fastened on him, in him. Worse, he knew also that he wouldn't remember this when he woke up.

But there were other things he would remember...

~

The sudden white light overcame him from behind. Maxwell could feel the radiance burning through the back of his head, searing his retinas, spilling out before him from the melting panes fronting his eyes. He grabbed the steel-framed Army Air Corps glasses away from his face, but he could still see his shadow stretching impossibly far across the devastated buildings and rusted automobiles.

Robert Maxwell scrambled down the rubbled slope with the rolling explosion lingering, low and gut-shakingly bass, in his ears. As the blast died, the bricks and broken paving shifted beneath his feet, some of the debris pulling loose and rolling ahead of him, each piece starting a small rockslide of its own. He almost lost his balance, but flailed his arms, catching himself.

This place stank of death. The odor was that of roasted meat, cooked far too long and then left out in the sun for days. Everything here was a shade of gray. All he could see lay on a monochrome spectrum between white and black.

Maxwell almost made it to the bottom of the slope before his sense of balance finally betrayed him. He sprawled forward, trying to roll and diminish the impact. The leather flying jacket helped, though his left arm started to bend the wrong way sickeningly as he put out his hand to take the fall. He felt the air knocked out of him.

He lay there in the broken stones, trying to regain his breath. His left arm didn't seem to be broken, though jagged pains shot from elbow to shoulder when he moved it. Maxwell tried to sit up. He couldn't find his glasses. He did find his USAAC captain's cap and clutched it as if it were a life preserver.

When Maxwell got to his feet, he turned and looked behind him, even though he had heard nothing. He saw what he feared. There were dozens of them, perhaps more, though he couldn't tell where the mass of shadowy stick-figures ended and the deeper shadows at the top of the slope began. They were raggedy things, tattered parodies of human beings. They moved jerkily as though infirm, and the first of them was already descending the slope. The figures moved perfectly silently, barely disturbing the rubble. In fact, Maxwell wasn't sure if his pursuers' feet were touching the stones at all.

Lungs and muscles protesting, Maxwell lunged away. He could feel the sweat cake the dust on his face. Panting, he forced himself into a stumbling run. Behind him, he thought he heard whispering.

Ahead of him loomed a ruined building. Something inside his head whispered, *refuge*. He didn't know why. But he struggled toward a dark doorway, hesitated, then entered.

There were no furnishings inside the hulk, just heaps of fallen brick and charred timbers. The room had one exterior window with a few jagged shards of remaining glass. Maxwell crouched behind one of the rubble heaps and tried to control his desperate gasping. He stared toward the window. He heard the sound of whispering, soft and indistinct.

Maxwell hunched down further behind his shelter, trying now not even to breathe, but still sneaking looks at the window. He waited in horrid fascination.

The shadow figures filed past the broken glass. Maxwell recognized the language of the whispered words, even if he didn't understand them. Japanese.

The last figure passed. The whispers died. Maxwell waited.

After what he estimated to be many minutes, the man slowly arose from behind the rubble heap. Starting to turn toward the door, he stopped in shock.

The little girl looked back at him from calm black eyes. She was Japanese. She was a beautiful girl, perhaps seven or eight years old. She wore a simple white shift and had a garland of fresh flowers around her neck.

The girl smiled at him, a shy smile, and then extended one hand toward Maxwell. The fingers were closed, but as they opened, the man saw they were webbed. He also saw what lay on the girl's palm. It was a netsuke, a small carved figurine. This one was in the shape of an exotic creature with a feline body and an elephantine head.

Maxwell recoiled a step. There was something—

The little girl said, "Baku?"

The single word terrified Maxwell. He didn't know why.

He looked down at his hands. They were wrinkled. He hadn't realized he was so old.

He wasn't old. He was twenty, and—

He was old.

The enormous bomber roared over him, props beating back the night. Maxwell blinked. There was no shining B-29 eclipsing the moon. What he saw was the plastic model on its stand near his bed. The humped gun turrets loomed in silhouette. What he had taken to be the whirling propellers were discs of clear plastic.

The bomber was going nowhere.

Was this a dream? Where was he?

He blinked again, attempting to orient himself. The little girl—

The bedroom door banged open sharply. He stared at the figure in the doorway. It was Marge, he thought. But Marge had died. How many years ago? Ten, Eleven?

"Daddy?" said the figure. Who was this? "Are you okay?" She swiftly crossed the dark room toward the head of his bed.

It was his daughter. "I'm fine, Connie," he said. He tried to motion her away. She ignored him, sitting on the edge of the bed and snapping on the lamp.

"I don't believe you."

Maxwell tried to force a smile. "I said I'm okay."

"Daddy," said his daughter, "I've seen more reassuring smiles on the bats I dissect in mammology." She crossed her arms across the USC nightshirt.

Maxwell propped himself on his elbows. "Thanks," he said wryly. "For this, I pay the university eight grand a year on top of your scholarships?"

"Give me a break, Daddy. You're not getting bad dreams from the raw fish we had tonight at the Pacific Palace."

"Could be," he said. "No reason dead fish can't have ghosts." He was suddenly aware his daughter was looking at him peculiarly.

"Why'd you say that?"

"I'm still half asleep," he said. "Look, I'm probably just a little edgy about tomorrow."

Connie smiled and touched his cheek. He felt the softness of her hand against his stubble. "Don't worry about tomorrow morning. This isn't the sixties. I'll bet the police won't drop gas from helicopters. Probably won't even bring dogs."

Maxwell said, "I'm reassured." He tried to stifle a yawn. It didn't work.

"Want some hot chocolate?" said Connie. She paused to cover her own mouth against a yawn. Then she pulled her blonde hair away from her face. "Mom always fixed me a cup when I had nightmares."

Maxwell shook his head. "Who says I was having a nightmare?"

Connie's voice was light. "I don't think what I heard was the dialogue from an erotic dream."

He stared at her. "What'd you hear?"

"You—" She hesitated. "You screamed."

Maxwell looked away. "I'm fine now. I'll be okay."

"This wouldn't have anything to do with the siting decision and the start-up hearing," she said.

He said nothing.

"I haven't been on your case about any of that."

"Which I appreciate," Maxwell said tiredly.

"I know this is a bad time."

"Yep." Maxwell wanted to turn off the light, keep her from looking at him.

"You probably don't want to talk about jobs and cheap power weighed against human lives." She smiled gently, undercutting some of the effect.

"Probably not."

She leaned toward him and kissed him on the cheek. "Tomorrow, then." She glanced at the clock and corrected herself. "Later today. We'll argue over breakfast." Connie got up from the bed. "I think very highly of you, you know."

Maxwell tried to smile at her. "I love you, too."

She stared at him a moment, then turned and walked toward the door. Maxwell switched off the lamp after she exited the bedroom.

He lay there quietly in the darkness, watching the red LED

digits gradually transform on the clock-face by the bed. Now they read 12:17. Beyond the clock, the model of the B-29 flew through the dark in perfect stasis.

In his head, Maxwell heard the distant, lingering thunder that accompanied the blast wave.

I'm dreaming, he thought.

⌒

The nightmare continued in the morning.

The clock read 6:41. Beyond the bedroom windows, the gray morning sky draped like a shroud over the San Fernando Valley. Maxwell eyed his image in the mirror, fidgeting with the final adjustment to his tie. He stepped back, shrugged, moved his shoulders again. The charcoal Armani suit had fit perfectly yesterday; today he couldn't seem to get it to adjust to his body. Nothing *looked* wrong. Things simply felt out of alignment.

Connie's voice drifted from the kitchen. "Three eggs or four?"

"None." Maxwell raised his voice. "Dr. Hansen's still trying to wean me off my cholesterol dependency."

He abandoned the mirror. Whatever was wrong was too minute to worry about. He must be nervous. That was it. He hadn't expected to be this apprehensive about the final round of hearings.

As Maxwell passed the shelves of netsuke on the way to the bedroom door, he abruptly halted, transfixed. *That wasn't there yesterday.* Had he even looked at the figures yesterday? Slowly, he reached toward the bottom shelf, his fingers stopping just short of touching the figurine he didn't remember seeing there before. It was carved from what appeared to be very dark jade. About the length of his thumb, the creature's body was feline, long muscles clearly defined, with a muscular tail looped around it. The head was that of an elephant, the trunk symmetrically curling to echo the tail.

He hesitated until he berated himself for being a chickenshit. Maxwell slowly picked up the netsuke figure, turning it over and over in his hand, the cold stone not warming in his palm. He saw no spark of life in the creature's open eyes, just the shine of polished jade.

Maxwell replaced the figure on the shelf and continued staring at it. He reached for one of the other netsuke. When he lifted the figure, he saw the slightly lighter patch where the dust had not fallen. He lifted the cat-elephant creature from its original position. There was dust beneath it.

"Daddy? Are you coming to breakfast?"

As Maxwell entered the kitchen, Connie set a plate of ham and toast down on the kitchen table beside a steaming mug of coffee.

"I probably shouldn't even let you have coffee," said his daughter.

"My heart needs the kick-start." He grimaced at the first hot taste of coffee, then set the mug down.

"Sit down," said Connie.

"Don't have time." Still with his attaché case gripped in his free hand, he turned toward the young woman. "Listen, quick question. Did you give me a present?"

Connie looked puzzled. "Not lately. Why?"

"There's a netsuke on the shelf I never saw before. Looks expensive. I thought maybe you knew something about it."

She spread her hands and grinned. "The Japanese art fairy?"

"No doubt." Maxwell took another draught of coffee. "The neighborhood's getting better if burglars are leaving expensive *objets d'art*." He checked his watch, then started for the door. "Sorry about breakfast, but thanks." He paused to give his daughter a peck on the cheek. "Wish me luck. See you for supper?"

"Can't, sorry. I'm going out with Paul. We'll probably eat down in Venice and then go to a movie. It'll be late. I'll let myself in."

Maxwell said, "When am I going to meet this mysterious young man?"

"Very soon, I think," said Connie. "Sorry, Daddy. He just keeps very busy."

"Me too. Okay." He smiled. "Have fun. Be careful."

"You, too," said Connie. "Don't let them get you down."

"The executive board of Enerco or the protesters?"

"Either one."

"Until I make some final decision," said Maxwell, "nobody's going to shoot me." He smiled to ameliorate the seriousness. As he shut the door to the garage, he realized Connie was still staring after him.

—

The Enerco Tower was located on Sunset, on one of the blocks where Beverly Hills segued into Hollywood. With its golden, reflective panes, the energy company shed radiance on its neighbors at all times of the day.

Maxwell squinted against the sun glare. Enough of the smog had burned away to the east; the Enerco Tower looked spectacular. A beacon for Americans. That's what the PR people were currently pushing as a catch-phrase.

Then he steered the Olds into the curved drive leading to the underground parking ramp and all semblance of peace ended. The walks were choked with demonstrators. He'd seen the placards the day before, and many other days before that. "Chernobyl, Three-Mile Island, Boca Infierna." "Power Now. Jobs Now." All sides were represented. Fairness in protesting.

Maxwell was instantly recognized. The penalty of momentary stardom, he thought wryly. The Board had wanted him to travel in a chauffeured company limo with smoked glass. He'd be damned if he'd be cowed into no longer driving himself in an ordinary sedan. Listening to the voices outside, looking at the variety of faces, he wondered if he'd perhaps made a wrong decision.

Pro-nuke or anti-nuke, the faces of the demonstrators ranged from concerned to furious. No one looked bored. Certainly no

compassion. A handful of company security officers tried with
only moderate success to keep the demonstrators on the sidewalk. Maxwell found himself facing several determined looking adults staring back at him through the windshield.

He lowered the window and said, "Listen to me, please get
out of the way." If they heard him, they didn't honor his re-
quest.

The press people were there, too. The reporter of a mini-
cam crew got close enough to shout a question: "Mr. Maxwell,
as the vice-president of development for Enerco, do you think
the start-up schedule for the Boca Infierna plant'll be set today?"

Maxwell said, "I hope so."

One of the demonstrators shouldered past the news crew
and said, "How's it feel to be a mass murderer?"

Maxwell ignored him. He was staring at a woman standing
perfectly still in the midst of the chaos. She looked Japanese,
perhaps middle-aged, though it was hard to tell. Her black hair
was combed long and straight down her cheekbones. The left
side of her face was obscured. She stood with fingers curled
into fists, hands at her sides. Her eyes stared directly back into
his. Maxwell blinked.

A demonstrator was screaming, "...killer!"

Maxwell snapped back into reality, almost as though from
a dream. Or is it the other way around? he thought. He stepped
on the accelerator. The Olds peeled rubber with a screech. The
demonstrators scattered as the sedan tilted down the ramp and
plunged into the underground parking garage.

The woman looked so familiar...but he couldn't place her.

Maxwell parked the car in his assigned spot and locked it.
He walked across the barren concrete toward the uniformed
company guard sitting by the bank of elevators.

When he was close enough, the guard called out, "'Morning, Mr. Caldwell."

"Good morning, Reuben."

Reuben had already punched the button for him. "Saw you

on the news this morning. The President thinks mighty highly
of you."

"The president of Enerco?" Maxwell said bemusedly.

Reuben shook his head. "No, sir! Of the whole blamed
country. Said you were a hero."

The elevator abruptly chimed and the doors slid open. Maxwell started to enter, then stopped in shock, recoiling. Dis-
tantly, he heard the clatter of the attaché case hitting the floor.

From behind him, Reuben said, "Sir? Something wrong?"

The little Japanese girl stood there in the elevator car. Waiting. She smiled and held out her hand, displaying for him again
the grotesque feline elephant form of the netsuke. The figure
glowed in the grasp of the girl's webbed fingers, casting a
white radiance.

"Mr. Maxwell?" Reuben had come up behind him. He shouldered past Maxwell, one hand unsnapping the holster at his
hip. Reuben surveyed the interior of the elevator. No one stood
there. No little girl. No one. "Are you feeling all right, sir?" said
Reuben. "Do you want me to phone upstairs?"

Maxwell shook his head violently and retrieved his case.
He got into the elevator. "I'm fine. Just fine." He was aware of
the guard staring after him until the elevator doors hissed shut.

At least the car was an express. He silently watched the
illuminated floor numbers mutate one into the next, listened to
the chime at each floor.

There was a janitor waiting for him at the top floor. The
doors slid open and Maxwell was confronted by a young man
wearing an Enerco custodian's coverall. He held a mop as if it
were a practice rifle at parade rest. For some reason, Maxwell
noticed it was dry. He paused, waiting for the janitor to get on
the elevator. Instead, the young man stared at him.

"Mr. Maxwell?" said the man. "I'm Paul Newton. It's really
important I talk to you." Maxwell realized how trapped he was
in the elevator car. "Mr. Newton, try an appointment."

Newton spoke rapidly, dropping the mop, unzipping the
coverall and slipping out of it. He was wearing clean, well-

pressed blue jeans and one of the "Chernobyl, Three-Mile Island, Boca Infierna" T-shirts. "Appointment? You know how
much chance there is of that. Listen, your daughter says you're
a good man—"

Maxwell felt like he was starting to slip into the rabbit hole.
He interrupted. "Hold on—you're *that* Paul?"

Newton said, "Yeah, well. I guess so. We've been going to
get together for a while, dinner, something like that." He smiled
cheerfully. "But it seems like you or I always have one meeting or another going on. I guess it's the penalty of being com-
mitted." He hesitated. "Truth to tell, I think Connie wasn't too
hot on the idea."

Maxwell tried to move past the young man. "Mr. Newton,
this isn't really the time—"

"Yeah, I know," said Newton. "Basically, I sneaked in here
to talk to you on behalf of one of the groups you won't meet
with."

Maxwell didn't know what the hell the younger man was
talking about. It evidently showed.

"PSC," said Newton. "People for a Safe California. We're
not loonies, Mr. Maxwell. Half of us want the jobs your
companies'll provide. But all of us figure we have a reasonable
fear we'll be fried in our sleep if anything goes wrong with
Boca Infierna."

Maxwell realized he was rising to the bait, tried to with-
stand the temptation to reply, couldn't. This was an objection
he could at least answer. "We're not talking Diablo Canyon.
The geology for the plant looks impressive. As for the safe-
guards—"

"Chernobyl looked fine, too." Newton tried to block Maxwell with the mop without actually touching him. "Listen, you're
a top guy in the free world's largest nuclear power consortium.
You've also got a family. You wouldn't want to lose 'em, would
you?" He sounded earnest.

"Is that a threat?" said Maxwell.

Newton shook his head violently. "I'm talking about what

happens if any number of your 'reasonable risks' beats the odds."

Maxwell started past his adversary again. This time Newton let him by. "I really do have to get to the hearing."

"And I really care about Connie, Mr. Maxwell. I care about her and me and everyone around us. I even care about you."

Maxwell hesitated. "I appreciate the concern. I'm not kidding about the appointment. We can talk another time."

"Count on it," said Newton, "but it's gotta be soon." He smiled at Maxwell, but concern sounded in his voice. "You'd better get some sleep tonight. You look like you need it."

Maxwell nodded. "I can sleep when this all is over."

"Good luck," said Newton. He stuck his hand out. Maxwell hesitated, then shook it. The younger man got into the elevator with his mop and pressed the button.

As the doors closed, Maxwell thought about sleep. What he needed was rest. He wondered if Newton were just as much a visual hallucination as the little girl with the netsuke had been. Perhaps, for Connie's sake, he ought to hope so.

—

This was real.

Isn't it? He thought, eyes blinking, staring around his black and white world, taking in the night-obscured field of rubble. He smelled dust in his nostrils. Dust and dead meat.

Maxwell half-crouched in the desolation, looking from side to side. He saw the heaps of tumbled brick, heat-blackened, the charred timbers and stubs of rebar protruding. Slowly, he straightened. He adjusted his Air Corps hat.

The spoiled-meat smell intensified. He heard the whispers.

Maxwell turned and saw the shadow figures contemplating him from the top of the slope. Their eyes were darker hollows in the blackness of their faces.

Hands that seemed little more than charred chicken claws extended toward him. The massed whispers raised in volume.

Isolated words seemed familiar. "...*hibakusha*..." "...*baku*..." He knew they were talking to him. He didn't understand, but he could recognize the tone. Pleading...Something else. The fear built in him. There were so many of them. They would surround him, envelope his body, bear him down into the carpet of cinders and ash. And then—

Maxwell turned and ran. He knew how exhausted he was. Yet his twenty-year-old body kept running, the muscles straining, protesting. The energy came from somewhere. Terror.

Clawing his way across the jumble of brick and stone, negotiating the maze of isolated, fire-blackened walls, Maxwell came upon the Jeep. For just a moment, he stared at it. It looked as if it had been there forty years. Some of the sheet metal hung ragged and loose form the frame. Yet the tires all seemed up, inflated. Without further thought, the man climbed into the front seat and twisted the ignition key.

The key? It's a miracle, he thought. It would be a miracle if the engine started.

The starter ground over and then the engine caught. It roared into life, the noise curiously flat, as though there were no echoes in the destroyed city. Maxwell jammed the shift lever into place, slipped the clutch, and felt the vehicle jerk into motion. The headlights illuminated the road ahead. He didn't remember turning them on. The bright cones speared through the dust, into the night. The road was a straight track. Somewhere far ahead of him, the headlight beams simply dissipated. As far as he could see, the road extended toward no particular horizon.

Maxwell looked back over his shoulder. Of course he could see nothing. When he turned back ahead, he involuntarily cried out.

The little girl stood on the road in the glare of the headlights. Maxwell hit the brake with his entire weight. The Jeep fishtailed crazily, slid to a stop with the front bumper not ten feet from the girl. Her dress was very white in the light. Maxwell comprehended the bright colors of the flower garland around her neck. The reds and yellows and pinks were the only colors here.

Dust billowed past the front of the Jeep, catching up.

The little girl smiled up at him earnestly. She extended her webbed hand. "Baku..." she said. Nothing lay on her palm. She turned her hand over, made a small gesture. *Down.*

Maxwell glanced down.

It was there. It sat on the dash where one might otherwise have placed a Bakelite Jesus or a St. Christopher's medal. The Baku glowed. Then it moved, starting toward him along the dash.

Maxwell acted without thinking. He reached, grabbed, hurled the figure away from him, far into the darkness. He could track it with his eyes, the increasingly bright glow trailing light like a falling star. His fingers tingled. There was something about his hand that felt good.

Maxwell screamed.

This time the sound echoed.

—

If being forty years older was a dream, at least it took place in a fantasy mostly quieter than the ruined, nighttime city.

Maxwell examined his reflection in the bathroom mirror. He morosely touched the deep shadows beneath his eyes, ran fingertips across the stubble on his jowls. *I feel so tired.* He turned away and walked back into the bedroom. He glanced at the clock. He was running late. It occurred to him that he was moving stiffly, something like the shadow figures that pursued him in his waking life. Wait a second, he thought. Do I have that right?

When he passed the shelves of netsuke, he abruptly stopped. Something was wrong. His vision registered the sight of something missing.

The Baku figurine was gone. There was only an indented ring in the dust to show where it had been.

—

Maxwell sat at the kitchen table, hunched over his coffee. He didn't have the suit coat on yet; it was draped over the back of his chair. He'd set his attaché case down on the floor by his feet. Connie came into the room and seemed to try to hide a doubletake. Maxwell knew he must look awful.

"Daddy," she said, obviously concerned. "What's wrong?"

"It's—nothing," said Maxwell. "It's gone, that's all."

"What's gone?" Connie poured herself a cup from the Mr. Coffee and sat down, scooting her chair in close to his.

"The Baku."

His daughter looked relieved. "It's around somewhere. I was trying to locate it in one of the netsuke books yesterday." She hesitated. "I thought I put it back exactly where I found it. Maybe not."

Maxwell held his hands over the coffee as though he were stranded in the Arctic and the cup were the only fire.

"The Baku's not exactly the prettiest of the netsuke."

"It's a household demon," said Maxwell. "I don't know which one. The Japanese have so many."

Connie said lightly, "Maybe whoever gave it to you broke in and stole it back."

"No one stole it," said her father. "I threw it away."

"An art object like that?" Connie looked a bit bewildered.

"It was on the dash of the Jeep."

Her face mirrored her sudden comprehension. "More bad dreams?"

Maxwell nodded. "Last week in psych we learned about night terrors. You know what they are?"

"No." Maxwell didn't look up.

"Kind of weird. They're dreams that linger a long time, even after you wake up—"

Smashed glass sprayed across the tabletop. The crash jerked them both back in their chairs. The fist-sized chunk of jagged concrete and rebar skidded off the table and thunked to the floor.

"Christ!" His daughter tried to shield him from whatever was going to happen next. Maxwell struggled to extract himself. They both stared toward the shattered kitchen window.

The voice from outside sounded like a bullhorn, the tone augmented and distorted: "Hey, Mr. Maxwell, we know you're in there. Recognize the debris? That's from the V.A. hospital in Sylmar. Souvenir. Remember how that sucker came down in the quake? So what's going to happen to your power plant a ways on up the Richter Scale?"

Maxwell and Connie exchanged looks. "Is that who I think it is?" he said.

Connie stared at him for a long several seconds. "I'm afraid so." She glared toward the window. "I told him not to do this."

"He takes orders about like you do." Maxwell stood up and walked over to the destroyed window. There were dozens of them outside. The usual placards were in evidence. He cupped his hands and raised his voice, "Paul Newton! You wanted to talk? Get your tail in here or forget it."

From the number of jeers that elicited, it was evident the crowd wasn't eager for a parley. "Okay," came the reply. "I'm coming in alone."

Maxwell smiled wanly. "It's dialogue out of a bad detective movie."

"Thanks, Daddy," Connie said. "Thanks for not calling the police."

"I may yet. Depends on how well your young man can talk."

Someone knocked at the front door. Taking the chunk of concrete-and-rebar in one hand, Maxwell made his way out of the kitchen. The window shards crunched under his shoes.

As he passed the hallway leading to the back of the house, he stopped, shocked. A woman stood in the corridor looking back at him. She was the Japanese woman who had stood in the crowd of demonstrators the morning before, the one who had fixed him with a silent stare before he'd driven down the parking ramp. Dressed in a somber jacket and skirt with a white blouse, she extended one hand toward him.

He saw her lips silently form the syllables, "Ba-ku."

Of course the Baku figurine crouched in her palm. He saw that the woman's fingers were webbed. He also saw the Baku glowing even in the daylight. It cocked its head and regarded him, the wide, round eyes shining even more brightly than the body.

He continued to hear the knocking on the front door, but now the sound rose and crescendoed like a long, echoing blast wave. The deep vibration made his teeth hurt.

The sound diminished and vanished. No one stood in the hall. There was no woman. No Baku.

I want to wake up. Maxwell shook his head as though trying to clear the remains of a particularly nasty dream.

The sound returned, but this time it was only the insistent knocking of clenched flesh on hardwood. Maxwell continued on to the door.

When he opened the door, it was, of course, Paul Newton standing there. He was wearing dark chinos and a black T-shirt depicting a fire extinguisher spraying a Bohr atom.

"Come on in."

Newton looked down at the chunk of debris in Maxwell's hand. "Sorry about that. Wasn't my idea." He grinned disarmingly. "You're in this game long enough, you learn to capitalize on the late breaks."

Maxwell carefully set the object on the hall table with the basket for outgoing mail. "Come on back to the kitchen. The fresh air'll be good for us all." Leading Newton, he continued, "I'm interested in your terming this a game, Mr. Newton."

"It's Paul, remember? I think we know each other well enough by now for that." His tone turned serious. "I don't think it's really a game, though it sometimes seems that way when we all get what it is—life and death." He seemed to force a smile. "Look, in all this, I'm not trying to find a fault."

"Pretty cute on top of your rhetoric about the Sylmar quake," said Maxwell.

"Sorry, things are heavy enough, I need a joke. This is serious now."

They entered the kitchen. Connie waited, pressed back against the sink. She looked tense. Trapped.

Maxwell said dryly, "I believe you two know each other."

"Daddy, I'm really sorry." To Paul, she said, "You told me you wouldn't do anything like this."

Paul Newton spread his hands. "It seemed like a good idea..."

"You promised—"

"Excuse me," said Maxwell. "Let's get to it." He sat down and pulled his chair up to the table. "What do you want to tell me, Paul? I've got to get to work soon. The hearings are moving glacially, but I think they're almost over. Tomorrow will probably do it." He shook his head wearily. "I hope to hell it does."

Paul Newton sat down on the other side of the table. Glass tinkled and grated as he moved the chair up. Connie walked over and stood at his shoulder. She started to touch him, but stopped. "This isn't the sixties, Mr. Maxwell. I'm not charging you with murdering babies with napalm or even conniving to blow up the world."

"Thanks," said Maxwell.

"That'd be unrealistic. What People for a Safe California are worried about are the maybe three or four million citizens who could get lunched here for the sake of your stockholders."

"I've heard all this before," said Maxwell. "I know you've watched the hearings on television. I think you're the sort who does his homework. How many times can we explain that Boca Infierna is maybe the biggest nuclear power project, but it's also the safest. Every time a plant's gone down before, we've learned—"

Newton interrupted disgustedly. "And maybe someday another power company will learn from Boca Infierna?"

Maxwell had no answer.

"I'm not willing to take the chance."

"When we finally work through all the clichés," said Maxwell, "there's no final answer. None. People want the electrical power. We need it. Enerco sees the acceptable risk as very small."

Newton said, "I hate phrases like that. Too glib. It's not an acceptable risk to me that any of us here could get wasted at any time just 'cause something or someone screwed up down at the plant and the wind's right." He stared Maxwell in the eye. "I don't want our kids to glow at night."

"Kids?" Connie said.

Newton turned his head and looked up at her. He nodded vehemently. "Yeah, children."

Maxwell said gently, "It's not as though it's totally up to me."

"But I think you've got the biggest single vote."

"I can be overruled by the Chairman, by—"

"Horseshit," said Newton. "Gonna use the Nuremberg defense? Just following orders?" He looked like he was debating whether to say the next thing. "Listen, I researched you. I know about your war record. I saw the UPI picture of you getting the medal for killing a hundred thousand people."

Wake up. Maxwell felt like sand bags were being loaded on his back. "That was another situation. That was war."

"I'm sure that was a comforting distinction to all those people who fried in Nagasaki."

"Paul—" Connie said.

"I was a bomber officer," said Maxwell. "I had a responsibility—"

"Yeah, responsibility. I'm frankly surprised a hundred thousand ghosts haven't hounded you to your grave."

The kitchen wavered, as though Maxwell were sitting at the bottom of a swimming pool, watching everything through a dozen feet of water. He saw the darkness of the ruined city begin to flow around him.

Newton's words brought him back. "You want to risk more? What's another few million phantoms?"

Connie's voice rose angrily, desperately. "Stop it! My father is a good man—"

"So was mine," said Newton. "You wanna know what happened to *my* dad? You may have seen it, Maxwell. There's a Navy base on dry land in the middle of Idaho. It's a government graveyard for faulty and experimental and deactivated reactors."

Maxwell nodded. "I've seen it. Pretty bleak."

"*Bleak?*" Newton almost spat the word. "I bet they didn't show you the human debris. People have died there. Not many, but if one was your father, that was more than plenty. Acceptable casualties, that's the term, right? The bodies got so radioactive that only a few pounds of meat and bone were saved from the autopsy for the casket. Everything else got put in a sealed steel drum and was buried in some waste dump."

"I'm very sorry," said Maxwell. "I had no idea."

"They won't even let me see where most of him's buried."

Connie put her hands on the young man's shoulders. He stiffened, but didn't twist away.

Maxwell said, "I can't say it any more eloquently, Paul. I'm sorry. I'm very sorry."

Newton rubbed his eyes and looked across at him. "I just hope you can deal with the ghosts, man."

The three stared at each other. Maxwell finally nodded. "I've got to get to the hearings. They'll go on whether I'm there or not."

Newton smiled for the first time since the front door. "I'll give you an escort through the lines. It's a sincere crowd, but not a dangerous one." He nodded toward the window. "That was a fluke. I'll pay you back for whatever a glass company charges to fix it."

Maxwell got up, shrugged on his coat, hefted the attaché case. He realized he was unconsciously straightening his tie and deliberately took his hand away from the knot. He said to

Connie, "Hold down the fort, love. I'll probably be late for dinner."

Connie looked like she was in an agony of decision. "I don't think I can be here tonight."

Maxwell stared at his daughter. *A nightmare.*

"I've got to go away and think," she said.

"Connie—" Newton started to say.

"Alone."

No one said anything else for a moment.

Maxwell felt the fatigue sweep over him. He said, "Will you be safe?"

"I'll be okay."

"Promise?"

"Promise. Absolutely." Connie tried to smile. "Maybe I'll call."

Maxwell watched her another few moments, then turned toward Newton. "Okay, son. Let's run the gantlet."

Connie hugged him before he left. "I love you. Don't have bad dreams, Daddy."

This is one. "I won't," he said.

She squeezed his hand as if she knew he was lying.

—

Of course he had a nightmare.

Maxwell dreamed he was lying asleep. Barely discernible against the night, a shadowy figure bent down across the head of the bed. A shadow hand gently touched the side of Maxwell's face. He tried to wake up, to confront the creature that was about to do—*something* to him.

The figure moved slightly and a bar of light from the window fell across its face. Her eyes. It was Connie.

—

He awoke from the dream for good into the night-time city.

Maxwell shook his head, attempting to clear it of the sleep fragments. He was sitting on a long, rectilinear chunk of concrete that looked to have been part of a building foundation. He stood and straightened his uniform jacket.

Maxwell stared as he realized what it was he was looking at. The wrecked B-29 thoroughly dwarfed him. Camouflaged in patches of muted black and gray, the sheet metal extended high above him. One wing crossed his vision to the side and extended far into the distance. Both huge engines on that side had torn loose from their cowlings, the prop blades twisted and corroded.

The man realized he was even with the cockpit. At that point, the fuselage was crushed down into the rubble so that the Plexiglas panes windowing the cockpit were almost low enough to touch, had he wished to. Maxwell reached out and gingerly ran his fingers over the panel below the cockpit. The metal was warm to his touch, as though the aircraft was heated from within. His fingertips traced the edges of the two black mushroom clouds painted in silhouette on the metal. Twin images. Identical victories. Two kills.

The silhouettes were abruptly hotter than his fingers could stand. He gasped and took his hand away, putting the afflicted fingers in his mouth.

Maxwell heard the whispering behind him. He also heard the voice.

"Don't fear him..."

It was the young girl. The necklace of flowers was still as vibrant and fresh as Maxwell remembered, the riot of colors startling in the monochrome world. She reached out toward him, fingers uncurling, revealing the Baku figurine.

"Please don't fear," she said again.

Maxwell stepped back, flattening himself against the B-29's massive fuselage. "Please, no..." He frantically looked to each side. The shadow figures leaned closer. Maxwell could now make out some of their features. He closed his eyes and turned away when he saw the man whose eyes had melted and run down the sides of his charred cheeks.

He opened his eyes and saw the woman who would always smile because of the flesh around her mouth and jaw having been burned away.

"Take him," said the little girl gently.

Maxwell stared as a shadow lengthened toward him from the Baku, just as if black ink were issuing from a spilled bottle. The edge of the darkness flowed down the little girl and crept across the intervening dust and broken stones. Maxwell wanted to run, but he looked at the creatures hemming him in and realized he simply had no further place to go.

He cowered against the crumpled metal and watched the shadow reach his shoes. It flowed up over the toes, then started to envelop him, moving up over his feet, up the ankles and legs to the chest, the neck...It didn't feel warm or cold. It simply felt like nothing at all. As the shadow reached his face, Maxwell was finally able to react.

"No! Damn it, no!"

With his fingers, he ripped at the shadow which had now almost completely covered him. The shadow-stuff came away in long, gossamer tatters. But the more darkness he tore away, the more new shadow flooded across him.

Finally, inevitably, it covered his face and eyes.

Maxwell heard himself scream.

—

He had once seen all three of George Romero's zombie movies at a USC festival screening his daughter had dragged him to one Halloween. Maxwell looked into the bathroom mirror and reflected that he looked a bit like one of the less colorful zombie characters. He ran the cordless razor over his cheeks again. He couldn't seem to get all the stubble ground down.

Finally he gave up. Giving his blue-striped tie one last tug,

Maxwell picked up his attaché case and walked to the kitchen.
He stopped short in surprise. The coffee maker was perking
happily away. Maxwell knew he hadn't set the timer. He noticed the place setting on the kitchen table. There was a note
rolled up in the coffee mug.

He picked up the note and smoothed it out. It read: "Daddy,
I had to see that you were okay, so I let myself in late last night
and watched you while you slept. I fixed you something to eat
and it's in the fridge. Just stick it in the microwave and nuke it
for about 30 seconds. I figure you'll need all the energy you
can muster today. I know this is the final day for the hearings
and it's make or break for the power plant. I'll be watching on
TV. I want to see you when it's over, but not right now. I hope
you understand. Whatever happens today, I'll still love you."

Maxwell convulsively crumpled the note, then flattened it
on the table, reading it a second time. Finally he folded it in
eighths and put the note in his coat pocket.

He went to the refrigerator to see what Connie had pre-
pared him. She was right. He needed the energy.

The morning cloud cover and a light drizzle dimmed the
golden magnificence of the Enerco spire. The weather did not
diminish the numbers of demonstrators. They all were waiting
as Maxwell wheeled the Olds into the circular drive and aimed
for the entrance to the parking ramp. The corporate security
people were forever urging him to use a driver, a company
limo, Enerco security escorts, different driving routes daily, all
manner of other security precautions. Maxwell turned them all
down. He wasn't about to be bullied. At least that was what he
told them all.

This morning he used the air conditioning and left all the
windows rolled up. What he saw out the driver's side glass was
silent, dream-like. It was like watching brightly colored fish

swim in an aquarium. Maxwell just stared at the signs, the rude gestures, the silent, frantically moving lips.

LAPD officers were on hand to keep the demonstrators from getting too close to the parking ramp. Maxwell had no trouble driving up to the incline and starting down. He parked the Olds as usual, locked it, and started for the elevator bank.

He realized with a small shock that Reuben's chair was vacant. "Reuben?" he called. No one answered. The echo bounced three or four times across the vast underground garage. No one else seemed in evidence.

Maxwell heard a burring sound from above him. He looked up. The overhead lights started to crackle and fizz. Then they dimmed.

He reached the elevator bank and pushed the "up" button.

The lights momentarily regained their brightness. Then they dimmed a final time and went out, starting with the tubes on the other side of the garage.

Maxwell watched the lights sequentially extinguished, the wave of darkness moving inexorably toward him. He punched the elevator button again. No bell sounded. Nothing happened.

Maxwell decided to try for his car while there was still light. He didn't make it. Total blackness descended. He felt a ringing in his ears. Lack of orientation clawed at him. He knew he was staggering, struggling for balance. He'd lost his attaché case somewhere. Carefully, he got down on his knees and felt around for it.

He finally touched the leather handle.

That's when he thought he woke up.

The lights came back up again. Maxwell realized he was still in the parking garage, but it was not the place he remembered from his dream, even though it was without color. He saw the Oldsmobile, just a few yards ahead of him. The car was covered with a thick coating of dust, the tires flat, the fenders corroded. It was part of the general wreckage that surrounded him.

Maxwell was still wearing his suit. Slowly, confused and

disoriented, he got to his feet, clutching the attaché case to his chest.

"Mr. Maxwell."

It was the Japanese woman he had seen first in the crowd of demonstrators, then momentarily in the hallway of his home. She stood not more than two yards away. She wore a simple white shift in the style of that worn by the little Japanese girl. She wore a garland around her neck, but the blooms were all wilted and brown. The flowers were dead. Her glossy, black hair fell straight along the sides of her face.

Behind the woman, the rank of shadowed figures seemed to stare implacably back at Maxwell.

"Who are you?" he said shakily. He gestured. "*All* of you?"

"My name is Mariko," said the woman. "You know who we are."

"I don't believe in ghosts," Maxwell said defiantly.

"Then call us what you will. We are *hibakusha*—'sufferers.' You saw none of us when you flew above our home." The woman's voice was level, the words almost gentle.

Maxwell said softly, "Nagasaki."

Mariko nodded.

"You must hate me."

"We hate no one now," she said. "We wish only to set you free."

"Free?"

"Of your past, your dreams. Set you free of your nightmares."

"By killing me?" said Maxwell. "I guess I can't blame you." The wind started to sweep across the rubble. Dust eddied up in front of him. He blinked.

"You don't understand, Mr. Maxwell. Listen to me. All we wish to do is give you this." She held out her hand. The baku was in it. As before, it glowed. Also as before, it moved, looking curiously up at Maxwell from her palm.

"Won't you listen?" Mariko shook her head vehemently.

"He does not destroy. The Baku is benign. You don't recognize the devourer of nightmares?"

"Devourer?" Maxwell said stupidly. "Nightmares?"

"He eats bad dreams. The Baku blesses any house with his presence, but only if he's accepted into it."

Maxwell stared at the creature. The Baku stared back. The man started to reach out, but then withdrew his hand.

Mariko said, "Please, Mr. Maxwell. If you cannot accept compassion, neither can you grant it."

He listened to her, considering that. "He will help with the bad dreams?"

Mariko nodded.

Slowly, Maxwell reached out and took the Baku from the woman's hand. The wind continued to rise, blowing the hair away from the sides of her face. The man saw terrible scars along her jaw.

"You were *there*," he said.

"The little girl was." She smiled. "I am not a ghost, Mr. Maxwell. Some of us didn't die right away."

Maxwell looked at her, then down to the Baku in his hand. The figure was warm. It pulsed gently. "He can eat all the nightmares of my life?"

"Up to a point."

Something occurred to Maxwell. "And if I feed him too many? If he can't—consume any more?"

Mariko smiled again, but bleakly now. "You don't want to know. Don't let it happen."

The wind wailed to a crescendo. Maxwell squinted. The light seemed brighter around them. Mariko's image appeared to diminish.

"Choose wisely, Mr. Maxwell."

The parking garage—*changed*. Color came back. The level of light rose. Maxwell looked beyond where Mariko had stood. The Oldsmobile was no longer a rusted, decaying hulk.

He felt the object in his hand. Maxwell spasmodically closed his fingers, then opened his hand again. The Baku lay there in his palm. It was the inanimate, carved object he had first seen on the netsuke shelf.

"Mr. Maxwell? Are you okay, sir?" It was Reuben.

Maxwell looked away from the Baku and saw the guard approaching. "Yes. I'm fine."

"They been callin' down for you, sir. I guess they really need you upstairs at the hearing." He gently took the tip of Maxwell's elbow and steered him toward the elevators. "Last day of hearings, huh? Bet that's a load off your mind."

Maxwell glanced again at the Baku. Then his fist clenched around the figure. This is the nightmare, he thought, isn't it? He wondered where Paul Newton was, where his daughter Connie was waiting in front of a flickering television screen. He even thought about Paul Newton's father, the several pounds that were left, resting in a sealed drum in Idaho. He wondered how soon it would be before he again saw Mariko, how long before the *hibakusha* whispered to him just outside the range of his vision.

The level of light in the parking garage continued to rise. Maxwell looked up at one of the overheads as the light brightened, igniting into a brilliance that blinded him.

The nightmare.

Isn't it? he thought.

THE
BAKU
A TELEPLAY

THE BAKU

FADE IN

EXT. - WIDE SHOT OF RUBBLE - NIGHT

This initial dream sequence should be shot,
as should all the other dream sequences, in
black and white.

The scene is an impressionistic place—a
landscape of ruined, rusted automobiles,
unidentified machinery, heaps of rubble.

In the b.g. sky there is a sudden white
light, a blossom of nuclear intensity that
grows and brightens until it washes out the
frame. There is the sound of a rolling, lingering explosion, low and bass.

The light dims, but we still hear the rem-
nant of the blast, which is joined in the
f.g. by sound of rocks slipping and falling,
the rubble shifting slightly.

                                    CUT TO

Robert Maxwell as he scrambles in a panic
down the rubbled slope. He is twenty, wearing a World War II flying jacket and an Army
Air Corps Captain's cap. As he reaches the
bottom, he turns and looks over his shoulder
back up the slope.

                                          CUT TO

The file of *hibakusha*, "the sufferers," at
the top of the slope. They are almost stick
figures, human enough, but thin and moving
jerkily as though infirm. Maxwell's pursuers
stalk down the slope toward him, eerily silent, somehow not disturbing the loose
rubble.

CAMERA FOLLOWS

As Maxwell turns and again flees. It has
obviously been a long pursuit. The man's
face is dusty and sweat-streaked, his breath
ragged with panting. A ruined building looms
ahead. Maxwell comes abreast of a dark doorway, hesitates, decides to enter.

There are no furnishings inside, just heaps
of fallen brick and charred timbers. There
is an exterior window with a few shards of
glass remaining. Maxwell crouches behind one
of the rubble heaps and stares toward the
window. He gasps for breath. Sound of whispering, soft and indistinct, from outside
the building. Maxwell scrunches up even far-
ther behind his shelter, trying even not to
breathe, but still looking toward the window.

Maxwell sees a line of shadow figures filing
past the broken glass. Sound of the whispering of the *hibakusha* registers with Maxwell.
Though the words are indistinct in *any* language, they are, in fact, Japanese.

Unwilling to leave his refuge, Maxwell keeps
staring at the blank, empty window until he
finally takes a few deep breaths and gets to
his feet.

Still keeping an eye on the window, he
starts to turn to leave and:

                                  SHOCK CUT TO

CLOSE - LITTLE GIRL

The little girl is Japanese, a beautiful
child about ten. She wears a white shift and
has a garland of flowers around her neck.

Back to Maxwell. He lurches back in shock.

The little girl smiles at him. It is a shy
smile. Then she extends one hand toward the
man.

The little girl opens her closed fingers and
we see the hand is webbed; we also see what
lies on her palm: It is the Baku, a small
carved Japanese figurine in the shape of a
panther body with an alien, elephantine
head.

Maxwell recoils back a step.

The little girl smiles again, once more offering the Baku to Maxwell with her deformed
hand.

CLOSE ON THE BAKU

It is glowing.

And then the Baku's head moves. It looks up
at Maxwell.

                    GIRL
          Baku?

CLOSE ON MAXWELL

He reacts in terror.

But now we clearly see that he is no longer
twenty years old. He is still in his flying
jacket and captain's cap, but he is dis-
tinctly the fifty-nine year old he is in the
present-day "real time" scenes.

                              CUT TO

INT. MAXWELL'S BEDROOM - NIGHT - CLOSE ON
MODEL AIRPLANE

a B-29 bomber. Pull focus past model bomber
to Maxwell, as he jerks upright and awake
from his nightmare. Sound of echoing cry of
terror receding under. Breathing heavily,
Maxwell lies back against the headboard and,
shaking his head, rubs his eyes.

FULL SHOT - ESTABLISHING

the bedroom. It is expensively but taste-
fully appointed, with individual touches of
both Japanese décor (a screen, perhaps a
Hokusai print, etc.) and a bit of World War
II memorabilia, such as a framed photo en-
largement of a B-29 in midair with a fighter
escort. There is a set of wall-shelves holding a collection of netsuke.

The bedroom door abruptly opens and Connie
Maxwell enters. Maxwell's daughter, she is
in her early twenties, wearing appropriate
college-linked sleepwear, such as a University of Wyoming nightshirt.

                    CONNIE
          Daddy, are you okay?

                    MAXWELL
          I'm fine, Connie.
          Everything's all right.

Concerned, Connie starts toward the bed.
Maxwell waves her away, but she ignores him
and sits down on the edge of the bed.

                    CONNIE
          I don't believe you.

                    MAXWELL
               (forcing a smile)
          I said I'm okay.

CONNIE
Daddy, I've seen more reassuring smiles on the bats I
dissect in mammalogy.

MAXWELL
(wryly; forcing control)
Thanks. For this, I pay the
university eight grand a
year?

CONNIE
(leans toward him)
Give me a break, Daddy.
You're not getting bad
dreams from the raw fish we
had tonight at the Pacific
Palace.

MAXWELL
Could be. No reason dead
fish can't have ghosts.

Connie looks at him peculiarly.

CONNIE
Why'd you say that?

MAXWELL
(slightly confused)
I—don't know. Look, I'm
probably just a little edgy
about tomorrow.

                              CONNIE
                            (smiles)
          Don't worry about tomorrow
          morning. This isn't the
          sixties. I'll bet the police
          won't drop gas from helicop-
          ters. Probably won't even
          bring dogs.

                              MAXWELL
          I'm reassured.

                              CONNIE
          Want some hot chocolate? Mom
          always fixed me a cup when I
          had nightmares.

Maxwell shakes his head.

                              MAXWELL
          Your mother was a very per-
          ceptive woman. Thanks, I'm
          fine. I'll be okay.

                              CONNIE
                            (hesitantly)
          Daddy, you know I haven't
          been on your case about the
          siting decision and the
          start-up hearings.

                              MAXWELL
                            (tiredly)
          Which I appreciate.

                              CONNIE
          I know this is a bad time.

                         MAXWELL
            Yep.

                         CONNIE
            You probably don't want to
            talk about jobs and cheap
            power weighed against human
            lives.

                         MAXWELL
            Probably not.

Connie kisses him on the cheek fondly.

                         CONNIE
            Tomorrow, then. We'll argue
            over breakfast.
                      (beat)
            I think very highly of you,
            you know.

                         MAXWELL
            I love you, too.

Connie gets up, shuts the door and turns off
the light as she exits.

Maxwell lies there quietly in the semi-dark-
ness. The illuminated LED clock reads 12:17.
He moves his head, eyes still open. Camera
follows the line of Maxwell's stare.

CLOSE SHOT - THE MODEL B-29

Sound builds, the echoing rumble of a distant explosion.

                                    DISSOLVE TO

INT. - MAXWELL'S BEDROOM - DAY - CLOSE ON
CLOCK

which reads 6:53. Maxwell stands in front of
the bureau mirror, adjusting his conserva-
tive tie. He's neatly dressed in an expensive and well-tailored business suit.

He hears Connie calling from the kitchen.

                    CONNIE (O.S.)
               Three eggs or four?

                    MAXWELL
               None. Dr. Hansen's still
               trying to wean me off my
               cholesterol dependency.

Maxwell makes a last impatient adjustment
and turns toward the bedroom door. As he
passes the shelves of netsuke, he abruptly
hesitates, troubled. He looks down at the
first shelf.

There's something there that shouldn't be.

Maxwell slowly picks up the baku figure,
turns it over in his hand. It is not the
animated figure of his dreams. It is just a
cold and artfully crafted figurine. Maxwell
replaces the baku and continues on to the
kitchen.

INT. KITCHEN - DAY

As Maxwell enters, Connie sets a plate of
ham and toast down on the kitchen table beside a steaming mug of coffee.

> CONNIE
> I probably shouldn't even
> let you have coffee.

> MAXWELL
> My heart needs the kick-
> start.

He takes a quick swig of coffee, grimaces,
and sets the mug down. He's got his attaché
case in one hand as he turns toward Connie.

> MAXWELL
> Listen, quick question. Did
> you give me a present?

> CONNIE
> Not lately. Why?

> MAXWELL
> There's a netsuke on the
> shelf I never saw before.
>   (pronounced net-ski)
> Looks expensive. I thought
> maybe you knew something
> about it.

Connie shakes her head.

Maxwell takes another draught of coffee.
Then starts for the door, pausing to give
his daughter a quick pat on the cheek.

                    MAXWELL
          Wish me luck. See you for
          supper?

                    CONNIE
                (shakes her head)
          I'm going out with Paul.
          We'll probably eat down in
          Venice and then go to a
          movie. It'll be late. I'll
          let myself in.

                    MAXWELL
          When am I going to meet this
          mysterious young man?

                    CONNIE
          Very soon, I think.
                (beat)
          Sorry, Daddy. He just keeps
          very busy.

                    MAXWELL
          Me too. Okay. Be careful.

                    CONNIE
          You too. Don't let them get
          you down.

                    MAXWELL
          The executive board or the
          protesters?

                    CONNIE
          Either one.

                   MAXWELL
        Until I make some decisions,
        nobody's going to shoot me.

He smiles to ameliorate the seriousness,
then exits.

Connie stands still, watching where he was.

                               CUT TO

EXT. - ENERCO BUILDING - DAY - WIDE

A cluster of pro-nuke and anti-nuke demonstrators have gathered at the parking entrance to the office building. As Maxwell's
car pulls into the drive, he is instantly
recognized, and demonstrators converge,
shaking their signs and yelling opposing
slogans.

From inside the car, Maxwell takes it all
in: the angry and concerned faces; the press
with minicams. The signs include:
'Chernobyl, Three-Mile Island, Boca
Infierna.'

Maxwell lowers the window.

                   MAXWELL
        Listen to me, please get out
        of the way.

One of the press people gets close enough to
shout a question.

                    TV REPORTER
          Mr. Maxwell, as the vice-
          president of development for
          Enerco, do you think the
          start-up schedule for the
          Boca Infierna plant'll be
          set today?

                    MAXWELL
          I hope so.

One of the demonstrators crowds past the
camera crew.

                    DEMONSTRATOR
          How's it feel to be a mass
          killer?

It's as though Maxwell doesn't hear. He suddenly stares directly at one woman who is
standing perfectly still in the midst of the
chaos. She is Mariko, a middle-aged Japanese
woman who might be older than Maxwell, or
decades younger. It's hard to tell; her face
is timeless. Her long, straight black hair
is combed forward on the side, so as to hide
the left side of her face. Her hands are
curled into fists at her sides. The instant
of almost-recognition ends.

                  SECOND DEMONSTRATOR
                      (shouting)
             ...Murderer!

Maxwell steps on the accelerator. Demonstrators scatter as the car peels rubber and
tilts down the ramp into the underground
parking garage.

INT. - PARKING GARAGE - DAY

Down in the parking garage, Maxwell parks
his car. He walks across the expanse of concrete toward a uniformed company guard and
the elevators.

>   GUARD
>   'Morning, Mr. Maxwell.

>   MAXWELL
>   Good morning, Reuben.

He punches the elevator button. The light
goes on. The elevator's on its way.

>   GUARD
>   Saw you on the news this
>   morning. The President
>   thinks mighty highly of you.

>   MAXWELL
>   (bemusedly)
>   The president of Enerco?

>   GUARD
>   (shakes his head)
>   No, sir! Of the whole blamed
>   country. Said you were a
>   hero.

Maxwell jams his thumb against the button
and *very suddenly* the sound of the elevator
chime peals and the doors slide apart.

Maxwell starts to enter the elevator, then
recoils, dropping his attaché case with a
clatter.

                    GUARD
          Sir? Something wrong?

Maxwell sees the little Japanese girl waiting in the elevator. She is smiling and
holding out her hand where the Baku rests in
those strange, webbed fingers. The figurine
glows as though radioactive.

The guard comes up behind him.

                    GUARD
          Mr. Maxwell?

Maxwell says nothing. He points toward the
open doors, looking as though he's seen a
ghost.

The guard shoulders past with one hand unsnapping his hip-holster.

There is nothing in the elevator now. No
one. Maxwell picks up his spilled attaché
case. The guard helps him.

                    GUARD
          Are you feeling all right,
          sir? Do you want me to phone
          upstairs?

Maxwell shakes his head violently and gets
into the elevator.

                    MAXWELL
          I'm fine. Just fine.

The doors close. Maxwell looks very, very
sober as the express elevator takes him all
the way to the top of the building with no
intervening stops.

When the final floor-chime sounds and the
doors slide open, Maxwell is confronted by a
young man in a janitor's cover-all, holding
a broom. This is Paul Newton.

> NEWTON
> Mr. Maxwell? I'm Paul New-
> ton. It's really important I
> talk to you.

> MAXWELL
> (trapped in the elevator and
> a bit confused)
> Mr. Newton, try an appoint-
> ment.

Newton speaks rapidly as he drops the mop,
unzips the coverall, and slips out of it.
Underneath, he's clad in jeans and one of
the 'Chernobyl, Three-Mile Island, Boca
Infierna' T-shirts.

> NEWTON
> You know how much chance
> there is of that. Listen,
> your daughter says you're a
> good man—

> MAXWELL
> (interrupting, suddenly
> putting two and two to-
> gether)
> Hold on—you're *that* Paul?

                         NEWTON
          Yeah, well. I guess so.
          We've been going to get
          together for a while, but
          you or I always have a meet-
          ing.
                         (beat)
          Actually, Connie wasn't so
          hot on the idea.

Maxwell tries to move past him.

                         MAXWELL
          Mr. Newton, this isn't re-
          ally the time—

                         NEWTON
                    (interrupting)
          Yeah, I know. I know. Basi-
          cally I sneaked in here to
          talk to you for the group
          you won't meet with.

Maxwell looks baffled.

                         NEWTON
          PSC—People for a Safe Cali-
          fornia. We're not loonies,
          Mr. Maxwell. Half of us want
          the jobs your companies'll
          provide. But all of us feel
          we have a reasonable fear
          we'll be fried in our sleep
          if anything goes wrong with
          Boca Infierna.

                    MAXWELL
            (rising to the bait)
        This isn't Diablo Canyon,
        Mr. Newton. The geology
        looks excellent, the safe-
        guards—

                    NEWTON
        Chernobyl looked fine, too.
                (beat)
        Call me Paul. Listen, you're
        a top guy in the free
        world's largest nuclear
        power consortium. You also
        have a family. You wouldn't
        want to lose 'em, would you?

                    MAXWELL
        Is that a threat?

Newton shakes his head violently.

                    NEWTON
        I'm talking about what hap-
        pens if any number of your
        'reasonable risks' beats the
        odds.

Maxwell starts past him again. This time
Paul Newton lets him by.

                    MAXWELL
        I really do have to get to
        the hearing.

                    NEWTON
          And I really care about
          Connie, Mr. Maxwell. I care
          about me and everybody
          around me. I even care about
          you.

                    MAXWELL
                  (hesitates)
          I appreciate the concern.
          We'll talk another time.

                    NEWTON
          Count on it—but it's gotta
          be soon.
                    (beat)
          You'd better get some sleep
          tonight, Mr. Maxwell. You
          look like you need it.

Maxwell's mouth curves, but it's a death's-
head smile.

                                        CUT TO

INT. - MAXWELL'S BEDROOM - NIGHT

The LED clock reads 11:56. Maxwell lies
asleep in his bed. At first glance, he looks
to be resting in perfect peace. Then we de-
tect Maxwell's eyes moving in REM under the
lids. He starts to toss restlessly. Sound of
Maxwell mumbling; we can barely make it out.

                    MAXWELL
          ...the *hibakusha*...I never
          meant to...

SPFX: Maxwell's image starts to ripple.

                              LAP DISSOLVE TO

CLOSE ON MAXWELL'S FACE - FRAME TIGHT TO
ELIMINATE B.G.

He is still fifty-nine, but again is in the
black-and-white dream, dressed in his Army
Air Corps cap and jacket. Camera pulls back
to reveal:

EXT. - RUBBLE-STREWN LANDSCAPE - NIGHT

Maxwell half-crouching there in the desolation, looking from side to side. Something
catches his attention.

Up the slope, the shadow figures of the
hibakusha loom up in the darkness. They
lurch toward him. Sound of massed whispering, a tone of pleading.

As Maxwell turns and runs, we see it's the
twenty-year-old Maxwell again.

He flees, clawing his way across tumbled
brick and stone. A parked Jeep is ahead of
him. It looks as though it's been there for
a century—corroded, tires flat, pieces of
sheet metal hanging off it. But that doesn't
matter to the desperate Maxwell. The Jeep
means escape.

As Maxwell climbs into the driver's seat,
the Jeep's headlights come on, cones of
brightness spearing into the night. He turns
the ignition key. Sound as the engine actu-

ally turns over slowly, tortuously, the
grinding distorted and echoing. Maxwell
tries the key again and again.

Maxwell looks up and reacts.

Ahead of the Jeep, the little girl stands in
the glare of the headlights. She holds out
her webbed hand. There is nothing lying on
her palm.

                    GIRL
          Baku...

She gestures down slightly. Maxwell glances
down and reacts, seeing the figure in the
center on top of the dash. It's where you
might expect a St. Christopher medal to be.
It glows. Maxwell grabs the Baku and hurls
it away from him, far into the darkness.
Sound of his cry, filtered and echoing.

                              DISSOLVE TO

INT. - MAXWELL'S BATHROOM - DAY

Close on Maxwell as he examines his reflection in the bathroom mirror. He looks like
death warmed over. He reaches up and touches
the deep shadows beneath his eyes, rubs the
stubble on his face. The pajama-clad Maxwell
exits the bathroom and walks like a zombie
across the bedroom. He's moving a bit
stiffly, a little like the shadow figures in
his nightmare. As Maxwell passes the shelf
of netsuke, he stops suddenly, registering
the *lack* of something he knows to be there.

The Baku figurine is gone. There is only a
clean circle in the dust where it should be.

                                            CUT TO

INT. - KITCHEN - DAY

Maxwell's seated at the kitchen table over
his coffee. The attaché case is beside him.
He's in a business suit and he looks dread-
ful. Connie enters the room.

                    CONNIE
          Daddy! What's wrong?

                    MAXWELL
          It's—nothing. It's gone,
          that's all.

                    CONNIE
          What's gone?

                    MAXWELL
          The Baku.

Connie looks relieved.

                    CONNIE
          No, it's not. It's around
          somewhere. I was trying to
          find it in one of the
          netsuke books yesterday.
                    (hesitates)
          I thought I put it back.
          Maybe not.

Maxwell hunches over his coffee as though he were stranded in the Arctic and the cup were the only fire.

> CONNIE
> The Baku—it's not exactly the prettiest of the netsuke.

> MAXWELL
> It's a household demon. I don't know which one. The Japanese have so many.

> CONNIE
> (lightly)
> Maybe whoever gave it to you broke in and stole it back.

> MAXWELL
> No one stole it…I threw it away.

> CONNIE
> (a little bewildered)
> An art object like that?

> MAXWELL
> It was on the dash of the Jeep.

Comprehension dawns on his daughter's face.

> CONNIE
> More bad dreams?

Maxwell nods.

> CONNIE
> Last week in psych, we
> learned about night terrors.
> Dreams that linger after you
> wake up—

Sound of shattering window and flying glass.
Both Maxwell and Connie react as a fist-
sized chunk of concrete-and-rebar smashes
into the kitchen and slams into the table.

Connie tries to shield Maxwell from
whatever's going to happen next. She protec-
tive, he confused, they huddle for just a
moment.

> BULLHORN (O.S.)
> Hey, Mr. Maxwell, we know
> you're in there. Recognize
> the chunk of concrete and
> rebar? That's from the V.A.
> hospital in Sylmar. Souve-
> nir. Remember how that
> sucker came down in the
> quake? What's going to hap-
> pen to your power plant a
> ways up the Richter Scale?

Maxwell and Connie, both huddled below win-
dow-level, exchange looks.

> MAXWELL
> Is that who I think it is?

Connie stares at him a long moment.

                    CONNIE
          I'm afraid so.
                    (beat)
          I told him not to do this.

                    MAXWELL
          Takes orders about like you
          do.
             (stands up and raises his
                    voice)
          Paul Newton! You wanted to
          talk? Get your tail in here.
          or forget it.

Sound of crowd muttering outside.

                    CONNIE
          Thanks, Daddy. You could
          have called the police.

                    MAXWELL
          I may still. Depends on how
          well your young man can
          talk.

Sound of knocking on door. Taking the chunk
of concrete in one hand, Maxwell makes his
way out of the kitchen and toward the front
door. But as he passes the hallway leading
to his bedroom, he stops, shocked.

Mariko is standing at the far end of the
hall, meeting his stare, a slight, sad smile
on her lips. She is dressed in the same non-
descript street clothes as in her previous
appearance when Maxwell saw her from his car
window.

CLOSE - MARIKO'S FACE

M.O.S., her lips form the syllables "Ba-ku."

She extends a hand toward him, palm up. Her
fingers are webbed.

The baku figurine sits in her hand. It
glows. It moves its head.

Maxwell had been getting it together; now it
looks like he's going to come unglued.

Sound of knocking on the front door rises
and crescendos like a long, echoing blast-
wave.

But when he looks again, Mariko is gone. No
one's in the hall.

Sound of a fist continuing to knock on the
front door.

Maxwell shakes his head as though he's trying to wake up from a particularly bad dream
and continues on to the door.

He opens the door and Paul Newton enters.

Newton looks down at the chunk of debris in
Maxwell's hand.

                    NEWTON
          Sorry about that. Wasn't my
          idea.
                    (wryly)
          You're in this game long
          enough, you learn to capi-
          talize on late breaks.

Maxwell shuts the door and leads Newton back toward the kitchen.

                    MAXWELL
          What would that game be, Mr.
          Newton?

                    NEWTON
                    (grins)
          It's Paul, remember?
              (beat, serious now)
          It's not really a game, man,
          though sometimes it seems
          that way. It's life and
          death. Look, in all this,
          I'm not trying to find a
          fault.

                    MAXWELL
          Pretty cute on top of your
          rhetoric about the Sylmar
          quake.

                    NEWTON
          Sorry, things are heavy
          enough, I need a joke. This
          is serious now.

In the kitchen, Connie watches the two men enter. She looks tense, trapped.

                    MAXWELL
                    (dryly)
          I believe you two know each
          other.

> CONNIE
>
> Daddy, I'm really sorry.
> (to Paul)
> You told me you wouldn't do
> anything like this.

Paul Newton spreads his hands.

> NEWTON
>
> It seemed like a good idea…

> MAXWELL
>
> Let's get to it.
> (sitting down at the table)
> What do you want to tell me,
> Paul? I've got to get to
> work soon. The hearings are
> almost over. Tomorrow will
> probably do it.
> (wearily)
> I hope to hell it does.

Paul Newton sits down too. Connie walks over
and stands at his shoulder, not touching
him.

> NEWTON
>
> This isn't the sixties, Mr.
> Maxwell. I'm not going to
> charge you with murdering
> babies with napalm or con-
> niving to blow up the world.

> MAXWELL
>
> Thanks.

                    NEWTON
          That'd be unrealistic. What
          People for a Safe California
          are worried about are the
          maybe three or four million
          citizens who could get
          wasted here for the sake of
          your stockholders.

                    MAXWELL
          (he's heard this all before)
          I know you've watched the
          hearings on television even
          if you weren't there. How
          many times can we explain
          that Boca Infierna is maybe
          the biggest nuclear power
          plant, but it's also the
          safest? Every time a plant's
          gone down before, we've
          learned—

                    NEWTON
          And maybe someday another
          power company will learn
          from Boca Infierna?

Maxwell has no answer.

                    NEWTON
                 (continues)
          I'm not willing to take the
          chance.

                         MAXWELL
          When we finally work through
          all the clichés, Paul,
          there's no final answer.
          None. People want the elec-
          trical power. We need it.
          Enerco sees the acceptable
          risk as very small.

                         NEWTON
          I hate phrases like 'accept-
          able risk.' Too glib. It's
          not an acceptable risk to me
          that any of us here could
          get lunched at any time just
          'cause something or someone
          screwed up at the plant and
          the wind's right. I don't
          want our kids to glow at
          night.

                         CONNIE
          Kids?

Paul turns his head and looks up at her.
Nods vehemently.

                         NEWTON
          Yeah, children.

                         MAXWELL
                       (gently)
          It's not as though it's
          totally up to me.

                         NEWTON
          But you've got the biggest
          vote.

                    MAXWELL
        I can be overruled by the
        Chairman, by—

                    NEWTON
        Horse puckey. Going to use
        the Nuremberg defense? Just
        following orders?
           (looks like he's debating
        what he's about to say next)
        Listen, Mr. Maxwell, I re-
        searched you. I know about
        your war record. I saw the
        UPI picture of you getting
        the medal for killing a
        hundred thousand people.

Maxwell looks taken aback. Like more weight
has been piled on his shoulders.

                    MAXWELL
        That was another situation.
        That was war.

                    NEWTON
        I'm sure that was a comfort-
        ing distinction to all those
        people who fried in
        Nagasaki.

                    CONNIE
        Paul—

                    MAXWELL
        I was a bomber officer. I
        had a responsibility.

                    NEWTON
                   (angrily)
          Yeah. Responsibility. I'm
          frankly surprised a hundred
          thousand ghosts haven't
          hounded you to your grave.

Maxwell recoils as if Newton's slapped him
in the face.

                    NEWTON
                  (continues)
          You want to risk more?
          What's another few million
          phantoms.

                    CONNIE
          Stop it! My father is a good
          man—

                    NEWTON
          So was mine. You wanna know
          what happened to *my* dad? You
          may have seen it, Mr. Max-
          well. There's a Navy base on
          dry land in the middle of
          Idaho. It's a government
          graveyard for faulty and
          experimental and deactivated
          reactors.

                    MAXWELL
          I've seen it.

                    NEWTON
          I bet they didn't show you
          the human debris. People
          have died there. Not many,
          but if one was your father,
          that was more than plenty.
          Casualties, that's the term
          right? The casualties' bod-
          ies got so radioactive that
          only a few pounds of meat
          and bone were saved from the
          autopsy for the casket.
          Everything else got put in a
          sealed steel drum and was
          buried in some waste dump.

                    MAXWELL
          I'm very sorry. I had no
          idea…

                    NEWTON
          They won't even let me see
          where most of him's buried.

Connie puts her hands on Paul Newton's
shoulders.

                    MAXWELL
                    (gently)
          I can't say it any more
          eloquently, Paul. I'm sorry.
          I'm very sorry.

Newton looks across at him.

                    NEWTON
          I just hope you can deal
          with the ghosts, man.

The three stare at each other.

>   MAXWELL
>   (finally)
>   I've got to get to the hear-
>   ings. They'll go on whether
>   I'm there or not.

>   NEWTON
>   (smiles)
>   I'll give you an escort
>   through the lines, Mr. Max-
>   well. It's a sincere crowd,
>   but not a dangerous one.

Maxwell gets up, hefting his attaché case,
unconsciously straightening his tie.

>   MAXWELL
>   (to Connie)
>   Hold down the fort, love.
>   I'll probably be late for
>   dinner.

Connie looks in agony about what she needs
to say.

>   CONNIE
>   I don't think I can be here
>   tonight.

Father and daughter stare at each other.

>   CONNIE
>   (continues)
>   I've got to go away and
>   think.

                    NEWTON
          Connie—

                    CONNIE
          Alone.

No one says anything for a moment.

                    MAXWELL
          Will you be safe?

                    CONNIE
          I'll be okay.

                    MAXWELL
          Promise?

                    CONNIE
          Promise. Absolutely. Maybe
          I'll call.

                    MAXWELL
               (to Newton)
          Okay, son. Let's run the
          gantlet.

They head for the door.

                    CONNIE
               (to Maxwell)
          I love you. Don't have bad
          dreams, Daddy.

None of the characters sees the pulsing glow
beginning to emanate from the hall leading
to Maxwell's bedroom.

                                          DISSOLVE TO

INT. - MAXWELL'S BEDROOM - NIGHT

The clock reads 11:57.
Maxwell is asleep, but not peacefully so.

Barely discernible against the night, a
shadowy figure bends down across the head of
the bed. A shadow hand gently touches the
side of Maxwell's face.

The figure moves slightly and a bar of light
from the window falls across her eyes. It is
Connie.

                    MAXWELL
              (mumbling in his sleep)
              ...Baku...

Using Technique, we ripple image and

MATCH DISSOLVE TO CLOSE SHOT - YOUNG MAXWELL

The 20 year-old Maxwell is dressed as before, as camera draws back to

EXT. - RUBBLE - NIGHT

Maxwell is still in the same black-and-white
nightmare world. He confronts a piece of
surreal metal wreckage that suggests the
cowling from a crashed WW II plane. Maxwell
reaches out and gingerly runs his fingers
over the black silhouette of a mushroom
cloud painted on the junk metal. The silhouette should evoke the "kills" emblem war
pilots have always painted on their craft.

Sound of the *hibakusha* shadow figures whispering.

Maxwell turns to face them. The little girl
is in front of the group. She smiles sweetly
at Maxwell. The floral garland is fresh, the
blossoms crisp and vibrant. She reaches out
toward him, fingers uncurling, revealing the
Baku figurine in her palm.

                    GIRL
          Don't fear him...

Maxwell steps back, flat against the piece
of wreckage.

                    MAXWELL
          Please, no. Not him.

                                        CUT TO

CLOSE SHOT - GIRL'S EYES

                                        CUT TO

CLOSE SHOT - THE OLDER MAXWELL'S EYES

Back to the girl as she proffers the baku to
Maxwell. As camera draws back, Technique is
used to show a shadow lengthening out from
the figurine, just as if ink were issuing
from a spilled bottle.

We see the shadow figures, the girl, the
Baku's shadow spreading toward the older
Maxwell (still in uniform), and the man him-
self cowering back against the wreckage.

The baku's shadow reaches the man's shoes and starts to envelop him, moving up over the feet, up the ankles and legs to the waist, the chest, the neck… As it reaches his face, Maxwell is finally able to react.

                    MAXWELL
                  (terrified)
          No! Damn it, no!

He rips with his fingers at the shadow which has now almost completely covered him. Shadow-stuff comes away in long, gossamer tatters. But the more he tears away, the more new shadow floods across him.

Maxwell's POV as the shadow covers his face and eyes. Sound of his scream as scene goes to black.

                                    DISSOLVE TO

INT. - MAXWELL'S BEDROOM - DAY

The clock reads 7:02. Maxwell stands in front of his mirror, adjusting his tie, his jacket, looking something like a zombie. He touches his cheek; there's stubble. Then he picks up his attaché case and walks to the kitchen, where he stops dead.

The coffee maker is perking happily away. There is a place-setting on the kitchen table, a coffee mug beside it.

There is a note on the plate.

Maxwell picks up the note and reads it:

>   CONNIE (O.S.)
>   Daddy, I had to see that you
>   were okay, so I let myself
>   in late last night and
>   watched you while you slept.
>   I fixed you something to eat
>   and it's in the oven. I
>   figure you'll need all the
>   energy you can muster today.
>   I know this is the final day
>   for the hearings and it's
>   make or break for the power
>   plant. I'll be watching on
>   TV. I want to see you when
>   it's over, but not right
>   now. I hope you understand.
>   Whatever happens today, I'll
>   still love you.

Maxwell convulsively crumples the note, then
smoothes it out, looks at it again. He folds
it and sticks the note in his coat pocket.

                                   DISSOLVE TO

EXT. - ENERCO BUILDING - DAY - WIDE SHOT

As Maxwell's car parts the line of chanting
demonstrators and starts down the ramp into
the parking garage.

Maxwell parks and gets out of his car. He
starts toward the elevators as usual, but
notes the guard's usual chair is empty. He
gets only a few steps from the car before
strange things start to happen. The lights

crackle and fizz and begin to dim. Maxwell
looks up at them curiously, and then starts
to run for the elevators as Technique is
used to ripple the image and

                              DISSOLVE TO

EXT. - RUBBLE - NIGHT

The older Maxwell, still in his business
suit, still grasping his attaché case, is
there in the nightmare sequence. It's all in
color now.

He looks around in confusion and notices
that his car is covered with dust, the tires
are flat, the metal's corroded. It's part of
the wreckage.

Mariko's voice comes from behind him.

                    MARIKO (O.S.)
            Mr. Maxwell…

He whirls to confront her. The woman is
standing a few yards away. She wears a white
shift in the style of that worn by the
little Japanese girl. Around her neck, the
garland of flowers is brown and wilted, the
flowers all dead. Her hair falls straight
along each side of her face.

Behind Mariko, the semicircle of *hibakusha*
shadow-figures stands silently watching him.

                    MAXWELL
                    (shakily)
          Who are you?
                    (gestures)
          All of you.

                    MARIKO
          My name is Mariko.
          You know who we are.

                    MAXWELL
          I don't believe in ghosts.

                    MARIKO
          Then call us what you will.
          We are *hibakusha*—"suffer-
          ers." You saw none of us
          when you flew above our
          city.

                    MAXWELL
                    (softly)
          Nagasaki.

Mariko nods.

                    MAXWELL
          You must hate me.

                    MARIKO
          We hate no one now. We wish
          only to set you free.

                    MAXWELL
          Free?

                    MARIKO
          Of your past, your night-
          mares.

                    MAXWELL
          By killing me? I guess I
          can't blame you.

Wind starts to rise in the rubble. Dust ed-
dies up.

                    MARIKO
          You don't understand, Mr.
          Maxwell. We would give you
          this.

She holds out her hand. In it is the Baku.
As before, it glows. Then it moves, looking
up at Maxwell from the woman's palm.

                    MAXWELL
          The Baku? To…to destroy me?

                    MARIKO
          (shakes her head vehemently)
          Will you not listen? He does
          not destroy. The Baku is
          benign. You don't recognize
          the eater of bad dreams?

                    MAXWELL
          Bad dreams…?

                    MARIKO
          He devours nightmares. The
          Baku blesses any house with
          his presence, but only if
          he's accepted into it.

Maxwell stares at the figurine, which stares
back. He starts to reach out, but withdraws.

                    MARIKO
          Please, Mr. Maxwell. If you
          cannot accept compassion,
          neither can you grant it.

Maxwell considers that, then slowly reaches
out again. As he takes the Baku from
Mariko's hand, the wind continues to rise,
blowing the hair from the side of her face.
We glimpse the terrible scars.

                    MAXWELL
          You were there.

                    MARIKO
          The little girl was.
                    (beat)
          I am not a ghost, Mr. Max-
          well. Some of us didn't die
          right away.

Maxwell looks at her, then down to the Baku
in his hand.

                    MAXWELL
          He can eat all the night-
          mares of my life?

                    MARIKO
          Up to a point.

                    MAXWELL
          And if I feed him too many?
          If he can't—consume any
          more?

Mariko smiles bleakly.

                    MARIKO
          You don't want to know, Mr.
          Maxwell. Don't let it hap-
          pen.

The rising wind wails to a crescendo. The
ambient light is coming up.

                    MARIKO
          Choose wisely, Mr. Maxwell.

                                    DISSOLVE TO

INT. - PARKING GARAGE

Maxwell is back in reality. The light level
continues to come up. The man looks down at
the Baku in his hand—it is the inanimate
carved object he first saw on the shelf.

                    REUBEN (O.S.)
          Mr. Maxwell? Are you okay,
          sir?

Maxwell looks up and sees the guard.

                    MAXWELL
          Yes—I'm fine.

                    REUBEN
          They been callin' down for
          you, sir. I guess they
          really need you upstairs at
          the hearing.
              (starts to escort Maxwell
                toward the elevator)
          Last day, huh? Bet that's a
          load off your mind.

Maxwell glances again at the Baku; then his
fist closes on the figure.

The light level continues to rise.

Maxwell looks up at one of the garage's
overhead lights as the light gets brighter
and brighter until it washes out the frame.

FADE OUT

                    THE END

THE HIBAKUSHA GALLERY

Hibakusha: collective noun; Japanese term, the rough translation of which is "sufferers." It came into currency following the atomic bombings of Hiroshima and Nagasaki. Though one hundred thousand men, women, and children died in the initial blasts, many more survived. Their wounds were not always apparent to the eye. No one can count the burned and maimed, the genetically blasted and physically mutilated. No one can total the presumably unharmed survivors of the two target areas who were ostracized by their fellow Japanese from surrounding cities. What use assigning a number to the survivors bearing invisible scars? Sufferers. *Hibakusha* labels them all.

—

I have a timer for the camera and I could take a self-portrait. But at a bargain price?

Here in the Amusement Arcade, the odors remind me of a childhood further removed than I care to admit. Winter's child recalling last summer's carnival: the heavy perfume of popcorn, warm and buttery and stale; the flatulence of adults drinking too much cheap beer; the shadowed muskiness of animals pacing hidden beyond frayed canvas flaps. The arcade is less temporary than my long-ago carnival.

I suppose some people could get bored here, but I never do. It's the Chinese curse about living in interesting times all over again. These times are fascinating.

The Amusement Arcade shares a legend with Times Square and the intersection of Sunset and Vine: at one time or another, everyone in the world will travel past. I believe it. People tramp in a continual procession past the clouded panes fronting my gallery. So many humans in the world now—and they all seem to visit the arcade. Sometimes I see familiar faces. They're not just tourists examining themselves in the distorted mirrors scattered along the boardwalk. They are my past clientele, drawn back by their fascination for the gallery.

But my old customers are outnumbered by the new. Some of them are forthright; they stride directly to the door and then inside. Others hesitate, glance at my displays, and then, apparently self-conscious, walk on. Often they circle the block for another furtive peek. A few stand beyond the glass, staring hungrily in like carrion birds. These days an increasing number enter the gallery after only the most cursory examination; impulse shoppers.

I've noticed that the demographics of my customers are changing—broadening, I think. I take note, but don't speculate much. Sales increase and the management stays happy.

And I remain capable of handling the days with equanimity, save for those mornings following my nightmares.

In my dream, I dreamed that my lover had died. And then, also in my primary dream, I awoke whimpering. My lover propped herself irritatedly on one elbow and asked me what was the matter.

What could I tell her? How could I say I'd dreamed we were making love, but when I had touched her breast, the taut brown aureole around the nipple had peeled away like dead skin, leaving exposed a disc of rawness that bled a clear fluid and felt slick to the touch?

What was the *matter?*

"Nothing," I said in the primary dream. "Nothing, nothing, nothing at all," until I rolled over and my voice trailed off in the down pillow. But neither of us could go back to sleep and she finally told me she wanted to make love. We had had sex twice the previous night; yet no one I've known could excite me more. I felt my body respond. Her eyes were colorless in the half-light before morning. Her voice was husky from sleep. Drawing me down, she said, "Touch my breasts."

Her irritation rekindled when I would not....

—

Though I had taken down the Closed sign, it was still early morning and no customers had visited the gallery. I hunched over a cup of cold coffee, waiting for a palmful of aspirin to take effect. When the door chime sounded, I didn't look up.

"Is it too early for you?"

His voice was low and husky, sounding more awake than I felt. I looked up at the man. "Too early for what? The gallery's open."

"I've known of your shop for—" The hesitation seemed deliberate. "—quite some time. I've wanted to see it."

I made a small motion with palms upward. The shop was here to see. The man looked at me uncertainly. I said, "Look around." His eyes flickered to the side as he stared past me. There was nothing in his behavior so atypical of my tourists, and yet—I felt vaguely uneasy about my first customer of the day. My clients usually come in after looking at the posters outside. Their eyes are trapped by the optical supergraphics and their minds by the subliminal voices urging them to "send home a truly different souvenir." Often their spouse and kids accompany them, trailing in like a covey of quail. Generally the first question is the expense of picture postcards and I quote the rates. Then the spouse looks at husband or wife and the other says, "Oh, go ahead, dear; it'll keep the kids quiet for a while and everyone back home will just be knocked out." They both will ponder the price while they look at the photos on the wall.

This morning's first customer crossed the deep blue carpeting to my counter. "My name is Daniel," he said. I reflexively introduced myself as he extended his hand and I shook it. Daniel's skin had a light mocha richness; his palm was cool and dry and reminded me of the skin of the python I had once handled in the Arcade's reptile enclosure. Snakes were never my phobia and so the touch fascinated me. He was tall enough that he could stare down at me, though I stand a head under two meters. His dark eyes looked out of a face asymmetrically framed by a bush of curly black hair.

"I'd love some coffee," he said, though I hadn't offered any.

"The what? Coffee?" Again without thinking I picked up his cue and turned away, fumbling behind the percolator for another chipped mug. I filled it and said, "Cream? Sweetener?"

Daniel shrugged. "If you've got it. Otherwise, don't make no never mind."

"What?" The mug pivoted like a live thing in my hand and, before I caught it, spilled tepid coffee down my trouser leg.

"You okay?"

I nodded. "Percolator doesn't make it very hot." I again filled the mug to the brim and set it down on the counter. "That thing you said."

He smiled. "Just an affectation. I said all sorts of regional things after I lived in the South. A few stayed with me." He sipped the coffee and nodded appreciatively.

I was watching but not seeing, nor listening. Don't make no never mind, her self-conscious irony. Leila—it meant "dark as night" in Arabic; but she was the opposite. She loved life and brightness; I saw that while she swam and rode and flew and made love. I had picked her up on the road in an Indian summer afternoon. She was bumming her way around the world. I was hauling baled hay for a suburban farmer. She stayed—too long.

The barren glare of the corridors absorbed her brightness; the antiseptic smell smothered her clean hair. She fought, but finally nothing had made any difference. She lay there in the special bed, connected to the attending machines, progressively weaker as cells by the millions cannibalized one another and died. Each day the fingers plaited in mine were weaker. Eventually she asked me to kill her. Pull the plug. I could not.

"...never mind, never mind," she said, finally bitter.

Again the dream died.

"Are all those authentic?" The sweep of Daniel's stare indicated the near wall of the gallery.

I motioned, paralleling the row of glossy atrocities. "Every one. If they weren't authenticated, they wouldn't be here. Look closely. They are Japanese masterworks."

"You sell these?"

"We have prints." I touched one painfully brilliant portrait with proprietary fingers. It was a twelve-by-twenty of what had been a children's playground, evidently quite close to ground zero. The three children had been vaporized by the initial blast. The heat had blackened the wall behind them, except where the children's bodies had absorbed the sear. Lighter silhouettes remained frozen. Shadow pictures. The shadow children pointed at the sky.

Daniel leaned close to the photograph. "God." I heard the pain in his voice.

"It draws a clientele."

He straightened and looked at me for a long moment. "Do you actually feel the cruelty I heard in your voice?"

For a moment I wanted to snap back the glib line: It's just a job. You get used to it. "No," I said.

Daniel turned back to the shadow portrait. "Nagasaki?"

"Hiroshima."

"I was there once," said Daniel. "I shot the complete port-folio to go with a text."

"You're a photographer?"

"What does it sound like?"

"I mean a professional," I said.

He pulled an envelope from the inside pocket of his jacket and spilled a half dozen slides out on the marble counter. He proffered me one; I held it to the light. I saw a bronze wall dwindling to a distant horizon. "The Downwind Monument," I said. I had seen it too many times before. I had read it, memo-rized a very small part.

Daniel said, "All thirty-seven thousand names." I must have looked at him questioningly. "Did you know they're listed al-phabetically?" I said nothing. From Daniel, a mirthless smile. "The neat aesthetics are spoiled each time a new name has to be inscribed out of sequence." I still said nothing. "And when there's no more space for additional names?" His smile now was genuinely gentle.

"Shut up," I said.

"Just a simple memorial," said Daniel, "for a small nuclear accident."

I detected no maliciousness in his words. Something in my expression must have signaled him.

"I didn't mean to offend." He looked away awkwardly. "May I see the cutouts?"

"The sets," I said.

"Yes, the sets."

I touched a button behind the counter and the black velvet curtains whispered back along the traverse. I depressed an-other button and the lights came up. I took a deep breath. "Aren't they fine?"

"You make them yourself?"

I'd wished I had, but I'm no artist. "They were fabricated by my predecessor."

"They are incredible." Daniel stepped close to the first and extended his hand, stopping short of actually brushing one fiberboard shoulder with his fingertips. He stared from one figure to the next. In his face I read an emulsion of horror suspended in fascination. I tried to gauge his reaction as he wandered among the faceless cutouts:

Nuclear blast victims, burn victims, figures of char and chancre. Men, children, women, flesh like seared pork, skin leprous with radiation lesions. All of them without features, ovals cut away so that other faces could be substituted. I can't say when last I had let myself look so closely at the sprawl of ravaged bodies, all linked in the anonymity of masklessness; all of them waiting for the vicarious participation of some customer.

"Is the process as simple as it appears?" said Daniel.

"Pick one." I wound my camera, counting the clicks until the first frame was set. I checked the light meter; then cocked the shutter.

"This." Daniel chose the cutout I privately called the Matisse. It was a chance parody of an odalisque, rarely picked by clients because of its inconvenient posture. Daniel took off his jacket, then lay down on his side on the carpet behind it. The set had been taken from a fire portrait, a photograph shot by rescue personnel moving back into the firestorm area.

The old man lay on his side against the juncture of sidewalk and wall, supported partially by a blistered, twisted elbow. His head was pillowed on a concrete step. What had been his garments and his skin were indistinguishable. He was still alive and not yet blessed by shock. At the end of his outstretched forearm, a hand like a charred chicken claw begged, as though for a cup of water or a sodden, cooling cloth.

"I'm ready," said Daniel.

"No," I said, "you're too tall." To smile was painful. "Your feet show."

He doubled his legs behind him. "Okay?"

"Great."

Daniel craned his neck, setting his head at the precise angle the old man's face would have occupied. "Still okay?"

"You're the perfect model." I went through the weary routine that had been taught me: "Now watch the birdie, and...smile."

"That I can't do," said Daniel.

"You aren't alone." The lights glared; the small muscles around his eyes twitched as he tried not to blink. "Sometimes they try, but it rarely works." I took a half dozen shots. "That should do it."

Daniel got stiffly to his feet, testing his limbs gingerly as though they were brittle. "Now what happens?"

"It takes a day to process the film and make up the cards. You want the usual package of a dozen? Fill out the slip and I'll have them mailed tomorrow morning."

"I'd rather stop back and pick them up."

"Whatever." I checked off the Will Call box.

He hesitated. "How's business?"

"Terrific."

"It's none of my affair," he said, "but as a professional I want to ask you. What did you do to get this job?"

Just lucky, I guess. "Nothing," I said. "Absolutely nothing. I just applied for the job, and I got it."

He gave me a tight bleak smile. "That's what I thought. I'll be back tomorrow."

"The pictures will be ready."

"You'll be here?"

I nodded.

"Then I'll see you in twenty-four hours. Take care, friend." As Daniel turned toward the door, something on the wall caught his eye. He gestured at the calendar pad. "When I left my hotel room an hour ago, it was still April."

I said, "Here in the gallery, it's always the sixth of August."

                                              —

I awoke disoriented and staring at streaked windowpanes, gray dawn beyond. My lover's face, drawn tight like a silk stocking across a skull, faded. The daylight had a texture and taste: cold copper metal clenched between my jaws. My tongue was dry and caked; sore where I'd bitten it. My head throbbed.

When I could no longer stand the feeling of damp sheets entangling my body, I got up and dressed in yesterday's clothes. Still not fully oriented, I stumbled and nearly fell on the stairs down from my apartment above the gallery. I entered a new morning, the sun not fully risen above the horizon. I walked along the boardwalk toward the beach and listened to the hollow cadence of my heels upon the wood.

This dawn the sea was quiet, the waves restrained. I slipped off my shoes and walked in the cold sand. The sky brightened above the ocean, but my mind was still night, pondering the eerie aesthetic of bombed and burning cities. I walked blindly, but saw an alien beauty: Guernica, Shanghai, Dresden, Hiroshima, Nagasaki, Quang Tri City, Haifa, Denver. The bombers fell from the sky like burning angels; the sea accepted them all.

Children's voices pulled me back. They were the only other human beings on this gray beach. Two boys and a girl, they played with their toy soldiers in the sand. One boy yelped and pointed to the sky: a white gull. I followed its flight with my eyes until it soared up into the east and full into the sun.

~

I don't remember returning to the gallery. I only remember sitting in my chair behind the counter and looking up as the door chime pealed and Daniel walked into the gallery.

"You look terrible," he said.

"I feel lousy."

"Do you want me to leave you alone?"

I shook my head. Without a word, Daniel made coffee for me. And then somehow, without deliberation or prompting, I started talking about my nightmares. After a while I stopped speaking because it had all been said. I checked beneath the counter and scavenged a half-full liter of brandy for the coffee.

We silently sat and drank and I contemplated him looking back pensively at me.

Then we both jumped as the door chimed. They trooped in single file—an early-venturing tourist family out looking for unusual souvenirs. All five were clad in bright beachwear.

"Good morning," I said, faking professional courtesy. "May I help you?"

The male met my eyes. He was a florid, hearty man who looked to be in his fifties. His sports shirt seemed to burn with flame-wreathed orchids. "Those cards," he said. "How much?"

The family proceeded with uncanny exactness to play out the scenario I'd described to myself the previous day. The five of them—the three children ranged from about five to fifteen—decided jointly on a family grouping. I shot an extra roll as a precaution against poses ruined by the squirming of their youngest. It must have been close to the end of their vacation: the father scowled, the mother displayed her own irritation, and none of the kids smiled. Part was my fault; there was little heart in my clown act this morning.

The father gave me a traveler's check and an address while I wrote out a receipt. His mood apparently buoyed up, he gestured expansively around the gallery. "I was a military advisor once." He grinned. "This is tame stuff."

I gave him the receipt and thanked them all for their patronage. "Nice place," said the man. "Really educational." He tried to give me a dollar back from his change as a tip; I put the wadded bill into his shirt pocket; he seemed affronted.

At the door, the middle child turned and looked back at the *hibakusha* sets with wide eyes. She said, "Are they really people?"

Her father answered: "No, they're dead."

"Unassailable logic," said Daniel after the door had swung shut. "'Forget the dead you've left....'"

More than once Leila had said, "I don't understand it."

"What don't you understand?"

"You were downwind too." She looked up from the sterile slate of the hospital bed, her blue eyes briefly accusing. "Why not you too?"

"I don't know," I said. "I wish it were me."

"No," she said. "Never wish that."

"I can't help it."

"No," she repeated. "It wouldn't help." But she rang for the nurse and told me to leave.

—

"What?" I said.

"Just a poet."

"I've had poets come into the gallery," I said. "I've had nearly everybody." I suddenly remembered the packet that lay at one end of the counter. "Here, the cards are ready." I slipped one off the top and handed it to him.

Daniel turned it over and over, examining first the side that showed the dying old man with his face, and then the opposite side with space for the address and message. "It's very professional."

"I'll take that as a compliment."

Daniel riffled the pictures as though they were a deck of playing cards. "Have you ever refused a customer?"

"Once. A man wanted to deface a set."

"How do you mean?"

"He wanted to cut an additional hole so he could expose his genitals."

"Was that so bad?"

I drew a breath. "The sets were mutilated sufficiently in life. In death..." My palms spread. "I drew an arbitrary limit."

"You do recognize the *hibakusha?*" said Daniel. "The sufferers?"

"Each day and night."

"And you don't recognize me?"

I stared. "What—"

"I thought it was very plain." Daniel shrugged. "Maybe not." He examined the backs of his hands. "There are no sores, no scar tissue."

I started to say a word but it stuck in my throat. "You?"

"I was visiting a city at the far edge of the downwind zone that day. I didn't *have* to be there—just a weekend trip to see friends. The doctors tell me I breathed at least eighty micrograms of plutonium oxide dust...not even enough to see with the naked eye." He looked at me calmly. "In the hospital they gave me a lung lavage to try to remove most of the particles; they pumped my lungs full of saline solution and then drew it off. Three times I was drowned, and thrice revived."

I said, "Then perhaps it was—"

"It wasn't. Some of the dust was encapsulated in the lung tissue. It's still there."

"Years have passed," I said.

He shook his head. "Even thanks to the accident, there are no actuarial tables for dust victims. The half-life of plutonium is longer than I care to consider. I don't expect I'll be waiting to see."

I said awkwardly, "I'm sorry."

He again showed me his humorless smile. "I didn't travel this far for your stumbling sympathy."

"Then why?"

Again the click and chime of the opening door; more customers. These were both young and beautiful; I guessed that they were still in their teens. Each was a creation of the summer: skin tanned to a rich shade of cocoa, hair bleached to drawn gold. They dressed expensively, were well fed and healthy. The two shared a youthful arrogance. The boy smelled of lime and oranges. I distractedly asked them if I could help.

"We're just looking," said the girl.

I directed them to the wall of photographs. Fingers entwined, the pair roamed along the lines of portraits. The examination was cursory. They returned to the counter where I stood rigid and Daniel was pouring more bitter black coffee.

I said, "Find anything interesting?"

"No," said the girl.

"What we were looking for," said the boy, "was something special."

"What's more special that you could wish?"

"Don't you have a scene with people making love?"

"The victims?" They nodded. "No."

As if suspicious that I might be holding out and concealing other pictures beneath the counter, the girl said, "Are you sure?"

"Perhaps you ought to try a straight porn shop."

"No," the girl said. "This is the shop we want."

"Then I'm sorry. I don't have what you wish."

The pair exchanged glances. The boy said, "Is there another gallery like this one?"

"None."

"Do you think maybe you'll be getting some more pictures?"

I said, "I wouldn't know."

The girl shrugged and took the boy's hand. She said to him, "Come on. We'll try somewhere else."

"Sorry," I said. "Maybe another time."

They left without answering, taking with them their fresh citrus scent. I slowly turned back toward Daniel, who was again shuffling through his deck of photo cards. He laid them out on the counter facedown in a Tarot configuration.

"But they're identical," I said.

"How astute."

"I don't need sarcasm."

"You need honesty." He shook his head. "I don't know what you need." As he had the previous day, Daniel pulled out the envelope of slides. "Let me show you something."

They stood framed against evergreens and snow; her eyes flashed blue like the clear winter morning.

I stared unbelievingly at the transparency. "Leila and you?"

"I was her lover long before you."

"Daniel?" I said. "Daniel." I shook my head. "She never mentioned you."

"She was too private a person."

I continued drinking Leila's beauty from the slide; my thirst had never abated. Daniel gently plucked her from my hand. Reflexively I reached for her. Daniel recoiled, his fist closing upon the transparency; when he opened his hand, the film was creased and split, the frame crushed. Blood gathered on his palm like a jewel.

"She's dead." I looked away from the ruin in his hand. "Why did she leave you?"

"She would have left you eventually. She wasn't a woman to be held." As I watched, he set the crumpled slide in an ashtray and lighted it from a pack of matches.

"You bastard," I said. "You didn't come here for the post-cards." The question was implicit.

Smoke curled briefly upward from the ashtray. Daniel took a handkerchief from a coat pocket and blotted the dot of blood on his palm. The sadness in his face was overpowering. "I shouldn't have come—not now."

"So why *did* you?"

"I took it upon myself to judge."

"Judge?" I said. He didn't respond. "Me?" Finally he nodded. "What for?"

Gesturing around the gallery, he said, "How you, a survivor, one of the few fortunate ones, can do *this*. I'd hoped to make you feel guilty that you survived. I was stupid. I failed to realize there was no need."

I recognized what was filtering into his words. "Don't pity me," I said. "Don't pity *me.*"

"All right," Daniel said. But his eyes contradicted his voice. And with the pity was a sick understanding. "I'd wanted to see what sort of man had loved her, and then survived her so badly."

I didn't reply.

"Such a luxury, self-pity. You don't use it well."

"At least," I said, "I'm alive."

He inclined his head as though to indicate I'd scored a minor point in a meaningless game. Then Daniel turned and walked out, leaving behind his pack of picture postcards. They remained on the marble slab of the counter.

"Hey," I called. "Don't forget your cards."

"I didn't." He paused at the door without turning. "Nor will you." And was gone.

I slowly sat down at my desk in front of the windows overlooking the ocean. I sat listening to the faint carnival sounds of the Amusement Arcade. I heard the tread of my potential customers outside on the boardwalk. Their footsteps echoed and deepened to a roar like the long march of waves tramping up the beach and then back into the sea.

I counted the waves and multiplied them into the days and weeks and years to come. Within each day is buried another night; and within that, the certain knowledge that I will live through it.

JODY AFTER THE WAR

Light lay bloody on the mountainside. From our promontory jutting above the scrub pine, we looked out over the city. Denver spread from horizon to horizon. The tower of the U. S. Capitol Building caught the sun blindingly. We watched the contrail of a Concorde II jet-liner making its subsonic approach into McNicholls Field, banking in a sweeping curve over the pine-lined foothills. Directly below us, a road coiled among rocks and trees. A campfire fed smoke into the November air. The wind nudged the smoke-trail our way and I smelled the acrid tang of wood-smoke. We watched the kaleidoscope of cloud-shadows crosshatch the city.

Jody and I sat close, my arm around her shoulders. No words, no facial expressions, as afternoon faded out to dusk. My feet gradually went to sleep.

"Hey."

"Mmh?" she said, startled.

"You look pensive."

Her face stayed blank.

"What are you thinking?"

"I'm not. I'm just feeling." She turned back to the city. "What are you thinking?"

"Uh, not much," I said. Lie; I'd been thinking about survivors. "Well, thinking how beautiful you are." Banal, but only half an evasion. I mean she *was* beautiful. Jody was imprinted in my mind the first time I saw her, when I peered up out of the anesthetic fog and managed to focus on her standing beside my hospital bed: The half-Indian face with the high cheek-bones. Her eyes the color of dark smoke. I couldn't remember what she'd worn then. Today she wore faded blue jeans and a blue chambray work-shirt, several sizes too large. No shoes. Typically, she had climbed the mountain barefoot.

Without looking back at me, she said, "You were thinking more than that."

I hesitated. I flashed a sudden mental image of Jody's face the way she had described it in her nightmares: pocked with red and black spots that oozed blood and pus, open sores that gaped where her hair had grown, her skin...

Jody squeezed my hand. It was like she was thinking, that's all right, Paul, if you don't want to talk to me now, that's fine.

I never was any good with evasions, except perhaps with myself. Survivors. Back after the A-bombings of Hiroshima and Nagasaki, the Japanese had called them *hibakusha*—which trans-lates roughly as "sufferers." Here in America we just called them survivors after the Chinese suicided their psychotic soci-ety fifteen years before, in the seventies, and destroyed most of urban America in the process. I guess I was lucky; I was just a kid in the middle of Nevada when the missiles hit. I'd hardly known what happened east of the Mississippi and west of the Sierras. But Jody had been with her parents somewhere close to Pittsburgh. So she became a survivor; one of millions. Most of them weren't even hurt in the bombings. Not physically.

Jody was a survivor. And I was lonely. I had thought that we could give each other something which would help. But anymore I wasn't sure. I wondered if I had a choice after all. And I was scared.

Jody leaned against me and shared the warmth of my heavy windbreaker. The wind across the heaped boulders of the mountainside was chill with the sun barely down. Jody pressed her head under my chin. I felt the crisp hair against my jaw. She rested quietly for a minute, then turned her face up toward mine.

"Remember the first time?"

"Here?"

She nodded. "A Sunday like this, only not so cold. I'd just gotten in from that Hayes Theater assignment in Seattle when you phoned. I hadn't even unpacked. Then you called and got me up here for a picnic." She smiled. In the new shadows her teeth were very white. "What a Godawful time."

That picnic. A summer and about fourteen hundred miles had separated us while she set up PR holograms of *Hamlet* and I haunted Denver phone booths.

Then here on the mountainside we'd fought bitterly. We hurt each other with words and Jody had begun to cry and I'd held her. We kissed and the barbed words had stopped. Through her tears, Jody had whispered that she loved me and I told her how much I loved her. That was the last time either of us said those words. Funny how you use a word so glibly when you don't really understand it; then switch to euphemisms when you do.

"You're very far away." Her voice was concerned.

"It's nothing." I fished for easy words and prayed for glibness. "The usual," I said. "My future with Ma Bell, going back to school, moving to Seattle to try writing for the Network." Everything but—*liar!* sneered something inside. Why didn't you include damaged chromosomes in the list, and leukemia, and paranoia, and frigidity, and...? *Shut up!*

"Poor Paul," Jody said. "Hemmed in. Doesn't know which way to turn. For Christmas I think I'll get you a life-size 'gram from *Hamlet*. I know a guy at the Hayes who can get me one."

"Hamlet, right. That's me." I lightly kissed her forehead. "There, I feel better. You ought to be a therapist."

Jody looked at me strangely and there was a quick silence I couldn't fill.

She smiled then and said, "All right, I'm a therapist. Be a

good patient and eat. The thermos won't keep the coffee hot all night."

She reached into the canvas knapsack I'd packed up the mountain and took out the thermos and some foil parcels. "Soybeef," she said, pointing to the sandwiches. "The salt's in with the hard-boiled eggs. There's cake for dessert."

Filling my stomach was easier than stripping my soul, so I ate. But the taste died in my mouth when I thought about Jody fixing meals all the rest of our lives. Food for two, three times a day, seven days a week, an average of thirty days a...Always unvarying. Always food for two. God, I wanted children! I concentrated on chewing.

After the meal, we drank beer and watched the city below as five million Denverites turned on their lights. I knew I was getting too high too fast when I confused pulling the tabs off self-cooling beer cans with plucking petals from daisies.

She loves me.

Funny how melodrama crops up in real life. *My* life. Like when I met her.

It was about a year before, when I'd just gotten a job with Mountain Bell as a SMART—that's their clever acronym for Service Maintenance and Repair Trainee. In a city the size of Denver there are more than half a million public pay phones, of which at least a third are out of order at any given time; vandals mostly, sometimes mechanical failure. Someone has to go out and spot-check the phones; then fix the ones that are broken. That was my job. Simple.

I'd gone into a bad area, Five Points, where service was estimated to be eighty percent blanked out. I should have been smart enough to take a partner along, or maybe to wear blackface. But I was a lot younger then. I ended up on a bright Tuesday afternoon, sprawled in my own blood on the sidewalk in front of a grocery store after a Chicano gang had kicked the hell out of me.

After about an hour somebody called an ambulance. Jody. On the phone I'd just repaired before I got stomped. She'd wandered by with a field crew on some documentary assignment, snapping holograms of the poverty conditions.

She loves me not.

I remembered what we'd quarreled about in September. Back in early August a mutual friend of Jody's and mine had come back to Denver from Seattle. He was an audio engineer who'd worked freelance with the Hayes Theater. He'd seen Jody.

"Man, talk about wild!" my friend said. "She must've got covered by everything with pants from Oregon to Vancouver." He looked at my face. "Uh, you have something going with her?"

She loves me.

"What's so hard to understand?" Jody said on that first picnic on the rocks. "Didn't you ever meet a survivor before? Didn't you ever think about survivors? What it's like to see death so plainly all around?" Her voice was low and very intense. "And what about feeling you ought never to have babies, and not wanting even to come close to taking the chance?" Her voice became dull and passionless. "Then there was Seattle, Paul, and there's the paradox. The only real defense against death is not to feel. But I *want* to feel sometimes and that's why—" She broke off the sentence and began to cry. "Paul, that's why there were so many of them. But they couldn't—I can't make it. Not with anyone."

Confused, I held her.

"I want you."

And it didn't matter which of us had said that first.

She loves me not.

"Why don't you ever say what you think?"

"It's easy," I said, a little bitter. "Try being a lonely stoic all your life. It gets to be habit after a while."

"You think I don't know?" She rolled over, turned to the wall. "I'm trying to get through." Her voice was muffled by the blankets.

"Yeah. Me too."

She sat up suddenly, the sheets falling away from her. "Listen! I told you it would be like this. You can have me. But you have to accept what I am."

"I will."

Neither of us said anything more until morning.

She loves me.

Another night she woke up screaming. I stroked her hair and kissed her face lightly.

"Another one?"

She nodded.

"Bad?"

"Yes."

"You want to talk about it?"

There was hesitation, then a slow nod.

"I was in front of a mirror in some incredibly baroque old bedroom," she said. "I was vomiting blood and my hair was coming out and falling down on my shoulders. It wound around my throat and I couldn't breathe. I opened my mouth and there was blood running from my gums. And my skin—it was completely covered with black and red pustules. They—" She paused and closed her eyes. "They were strangely beautiful." She whimpered. "The worst—" She clung to me tightly. "Oh God! The worst part was that I was pregnant."

She roughly pushed herself away and wouldn't let me try to comfort her. She lay on her back and stared at the ceiling. Finally, childlike, she took my hand. She held my fingers very tight all the rest of the night.

She loves me not.

But she did, I thought. She does. In her own way, just like you love her. It's never going to be like you imagined it as a kid. But you love her. Ask her. Ask her now.

"What's going on?" Jody asked, craning her neck to look directly below our ledge. Far down we saw a pair of headlights, a car sliding around the hairpin turns in the foothills road. The whine of a racing turbine rasped our ears.

"I don't know. Some clown in a hurry to park with his girl."

The car approached the crest of a hill and for an instant the driving-lights shone directly at us, dazzling our eyes. Jody jerked back and screamed. "The sun! So bright! God, Pittsburgh—" Her strength seemed to drain; I lowered her gently to the ledge and sat down beside her. The rock was rough and cold as the day's heat left. I couldn't see Jody's face, except as a blur in the darkness. There was light from the city and a little from the stars, but the moon hadn't risen.

"Please kiss me."

I kissed her and used the forbidden words.

"I love you."

I touched her breast; she shivered against me and whispered something I couldn't quite understand. A while later my hand touched the waist of her jeans and she drew away.

"Paul, no."

"Why not?" The beer and my emotional jag pulsed in the back of my skull. I ached.

"You know."

I knew. For a while she didn't say anything more, nor did I. We felt tension build its barrier. Then she relaxed and put her cheek against mine. Somehow we both laughed and the tension eased.

Ask her. And I knew I couldn't delay longer. "Damn it," I said, "I still love you. And I know what I'm getting into." I paused to breathe. "After Christmas I'm taking off for Seattle. I want you to marry me there."

I felt her muscles tense. Jody pulled away from me and got to her feet. She walked to the end of the ledge and looked out beyond the city. She turned to face me and her hands were clenched.

"I don't know," she said. "At the end of summer I'd have said no immediately. Now—"

I sat silent.

"We'd better go," she said after a while, her voice calm and even. "It's very late."

We climbed down from the rocks then, with the November chill a well of silence between us.